SEPARATE CABINS

JANET DAILEY

Harlequin Books

TORONTO • NEW YORK • LONDON
AMSTERDAM • PARIS • SYDNEY • HAMBURG
STOCKHOLM • ATHENS • TOKYO • MILAN

First published by Silhouette Books 1983

ISBN 0-373-15192-6

© *Janet Dailey 1983*

® *are Trademarks registered in the United States Patent and Trademark Office and in other countries.*

Printed in U.S.A.

ACKNOWLEDGMENTS

We wish to offer a special thanks to the Princess Cruise Lines for their cooperation and assistance during our research on their ship, the *Pacific Princess,* on its cruise to the Mexican Riviera. And a special acknowledgment, too, goes to Max Hall with the Princess Cruise Lines for his assistance. It was greatly appreciated. Lastly, we'd like to thank Captain John Young and the crew of the *Pacific Princess* for practically allowing us the run of the ship. We enjoyed his company immensely and especially his wonderful British wit.

BILL and JANET DAILEY

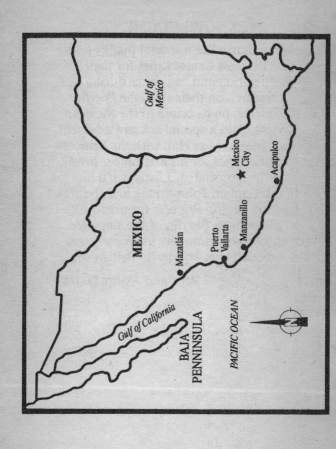

CHAPTER ONE

"IT WILL be approximately another twenty minutes before they'll begin boarding passengers. You'll be going through that door." The young woman, seated behind the table, pointed to the open doorway at the far end of the cavernous port terminal, then passed Rachel a long, narrow boarding card and two visitor passes. "Enjoy your cruise, Mrs. MacKinley."

"Thank you." Rachel stepped away from the table to make room for the next passenger in line, then paused to look around and locate the couple who had come to see her off.

The long table was one of several that had been set up to process the tickets and papers of arriving cruise passengers. Their location split the long half of the huge room nearly in the middle, separating the waiting area with seats from the baggage-handling section where passengers' luggage was loaded on a conveyer belt and carried out to the ship's hold. From there the luggage would be disbursed to the cabins indicated on their attached tags and be waiting in the passengers' assigned rooms when they came aboard.

The sitting area did not have enough seats to accommodate all of the hundreds of waiting passengers gathered in the terminal building of the port of Los Angeles. The size of the crowd was increased by the addition of friends or relatives who accompanied some of the passengers, like Rachel. The majority of the passengers and their guests were milling around the large open area near the entrance. Somewhere in that throng of people were Rachel's friends, Fan and John Kemper.

As Rachel moved toward the crowd her gray eyes made a slow, searching sweep of the faces, but it was the red-flowered silk of her friend's shirtwaist dress that caught her attention and guided Rachel to the waiting couple.

"Everything all set?" John Kemper inquired as Rachel rejoined them.

By profession he was an attorney, of medium height and blond hair thinning to show the start of a bald spot at the back of his head. On the weekends he avoided the conservative dress of his profession in favor of flashier garb, like the loud red slacks and plaid blazer he was wearing. Mac MacKinley had been a client of his. It was through that association and Rachel's long-time friendship with John's wife that she had met Mac, later marrying him.

"Everything is set," Rachel confirmed and handed him the two visitor cards. "Here are your passes. After all the passengers are on board, they'll let the visitors on the ship...which we won't board for another twenty minutes."

"If that's the case, let's wait outside," Fan suggested immediately. "It's so crowded and noisy in here that I can hardly hear myself think."

As Fan spoke Rachel was accidentally jostled by the person next to her, giving credence to her friend's suggestion. "Lead the way," she agreed.

John headed their exodus, threading a path through the press of milling people to the door. Single file, the two women followed after him with Rachel bringing up the rear. A faint smile touched the corners of her mouth at the way Fan kept glancing over her shoulder to be sure Rachel was behind them. It was a mother-hen trait that came naturally to Fan, accustomed to keeping track of her brood of four children, three boys and a much awaited girl.

The thought of the four towheaded youngsters brought a flicker of remorse, sobering the gray of her eyes. More than once in the last four years Rachel had wished she and Mac hadn't decided to wait awhile before starting a family. At the time it had seemed sensible, since their furniture business was expanding with branch stores. Mac had been such a big, strapping man, so full of life and ambition. No one could have foretold that a massive coronary would take his life before he turned thirty-five.

They passed out of the building's shade into the slanting sunlight of a February afternoon. A drifting breeze picked up the scent of flowers from the bouquets for sale as bon voyage gifts just outside the terminal's entrance. Rachel made an effort to throw off those reflective thoughts of the past and look to the present and its surroundings.

A few other people shared their desire to escape the crowd inside the building and dawdled on the walk, watching the late arrivals as they drove up to the curb. A long row of buses was parked to one side, having already transported those passengers who had flown into the Los Angeles airport.

"We can sit over here on this ledge." Fan led them to a landscaped island of palms and shrubbery where there was room for them to sit on the concrete lip of the low wall.

Conscious of how quickly the skirt of her white suit showed the smallest trace of dust or dirt, Rachel brushed at the seat before she sat down. The femininely tailored suit was a flattering choice, showing the slimness of her long-legged figure. Its whiteness accented the ebony sheen of her black hair and the silvery lightness of her gray eyes, sooted in with dark, curling lashes. Her blouse was a jewel-bright shade of blue silk with a collar that tied into a wide bow. It was a striking outfit, made all the more stunning by the attractive beauty of the woman wearing it.

John remained standing, not taking a seat on the ledge beside them. "There's a catering truck parked down the way. Would you girls like something cold to drink?"

"I'll have a diet cola." Fan was quick to accept her husband's offer, then glanced inquiringly at Rachel. "Rachel?"

"An orange drink, please."

"A diet cola and an orange drink coming right up," John repeated their orders, then sketched them a brief salute before moving away.

There was a thoughtful smile on Fan's face as she watched her husband leave. After a second she turned to Rachel and sighed, "I love it when he calls us 'girls.' It makes me feel as if I'm eighteen again." She laughed shortly, a merry sound full of fun at herself. "Half the time I think I still am. That is"—she qualified—"until those four little demons of mine come charging into our bedroom in the mornings. Then I'm forced to remember I passed the thirty mark two years ago."

"You look the same as you did the day we graduated from college," Rachel insisted, but made no comment about Fan's reference to her children. The mention of them came too quickly after her own thoughts of regret for her childless existence.

"Then how come the red dress I wore that day clings in all the wrong places when I try to wear it now?" Fan demanded with a mocking look. "I suppose after four children I should be grateful I can get into it at all."

"You look wonderful and you know it," Rachel assured her friend, because it was true.

There were minor changes in Fan's appearance. Her blonde hair no longer flowed silkenly to her waist; it was shorter and styled in a sophisticated French sweep. Her once pencil-thin figure was now well rounded but still slender. And Fan was the same person, actively involved in a half dozen projects at once and managing to successfully juggle them all. The quickest way to make an enemy of her was by still calling her Fanny instead of Fan, an appellation she hated.

"I look like exactly what I am—a country club mother of four children, wife of a successful attorney with a flourishing law practice, and committee member of a dozen charities. All the conventional things I vowed I would never be...until I met John. And I couldn't be happier and more fulfilled than I am now," she declared with a serenely contented smile.

"Sometimes I wonder where the years have gone." Rachel turned her wistful gray eyes to the pale blue sky and stared, lost in its infinity. "Graduation seems like only yesterday. I turn around, and here I am—thirty-two years old and—" She had been about to say "alone," but she stopped herself.

"And about to embark on a glorious seven-day cruise down the Mexican Riviera," Fan finished the sentence for her, deliberately steering it away from any potentially depressing thought.

Recognizing her friend's intention, Rachel swung her gaze around and smiled in silent gratitude of Fan's understanding. "I don't actually believe I'm going yet," she admitted with a touch of wryness. "I probably won't believe it until the ship leaves and I'm on it."

Her comment seemed to explain her lack of enthusiasm. She'd planned vacations before, but something had always come up at the last minute, forcing her to cancel. A small frown of concentration lay upon her features as Rachel mentally went over her checklist to see if she had overlooked any item that might now crop up.

"This time you're going," Fan stated. "John and I are personally going to make certain you are on the *Pacific Princess* when she leaves. After all I went through making the reservations and picking up your ticket last week, you're going."

Rachel smiled absently at the firm avowal. Something was nagging at her, holding any eager anticipation for the trip at bay. It darkened her gray eyes, giving them a vaguely troubled and faraway look.

"You could look a little more excited," her friend accused.

"Sorry." She flashed a glance at Fan, still slightly preoccupied. "I have this feeling I've forgotten something."

"I don't know what it could be." Now it was the blonde who frowned as she considered the possibilities. "Mrs. Pollock, next door, already has the key so she can water your houseplants. And you've arranged to have your mail held at the post office until you come back. You did check to make sure your passport hasn't expired, didn't you?"

"It's current," Rachel nodded. Even without it she had enough other identification with her to allow her to enter and leave Mexico.

"Everything else has been handled, and they've already taken your luggage aboard." Fan sighed and briefly shook her head. "I can't think of anything other than that."

"Other than what?" John returned with their cold drinks in time to catch the last part of his wife's remark. His fingers were splayed to grip the three containers, slippery with the condensation coating their sides. Plastic straws were poking out of their tops.

"Rachel thinks she's forgotten something," Fan explained as she took two of the drinks from him before John dropped them, and passed the orange soda to Rachel.

"She has," he stated without hesitation and reached in the side pocket of his plaid blazer to offer them napkins.

"What?" Her gray eyes widened, surprised that he seemed to know something she didn't.

"The cares of the world," he pronounced, then let a knowing little smile curve his mouth. "Or more specifically, the care of the Country House, home of fine furniture. Which is the same thing since you've made it your whole world after you lost Mac."

"I wouldn't say it's my *whole* world." Rachel was obliged to protest his all-inclusive assessment, yet she realised it was true.

The furniture company had almost become the child she and Mac never had, the recipient of her time and attention. In the last four years since Mac's death she had lost touch with most of the friends who were outside her business sphere—with the exception of Fan. Even then, the close contact had been maintained mostly because John acted as both her business and personal attorney. Nearly everything in her life revolved around the company and its stores.

Fortunately she had worked in the company, both at the retail outlets and in the office, putting to practical use her college degree in business management, after she and Mac were married, so she'd had the knowledge and experience to run it herself when she had acquired sole ownership of it on his death. It hadn't been easy, but the challenge of putting the company on a more solid footing had been rewarding, both emotionally and monetarily. She'd had the satisfaction of taking something she and Mac had dreamed and making it come true.

"For all intents and purposes it might as well be," John countered, knowing her too well.

"Perhaps," Rachel conceded absently. His reference to the business had unrolled a new string of thoughts. She lifted back the cuff of her jacket sleeve and glanced at the thin gold watch around her wrist. "I should be able to catch Ben Atkins at the office. I have time before they begin boarding passengers, so I think I'd better phone him. That ad campaign is going to start running on television next and I need—"

"You are not going to call anybody." Fan laid a restraining hand on her arm, firmly asserting an authority born of friendship. "You are staying right here. I'm not going to let a last-minute phone call interfere with your vacation plans."

"This is not the most opportune time to be gone for two weeks." As soon as she said it Rachel recognized it was this knowledge that had been troubling her. She began to have doubts about the wisdom of leaving on the cruise just at the launch of a major ad campaign. Granted, the cruise only lasted seven days, but she had planned on staying in Acapulco a few days longer before flying back. Of course, she could always cut short that stay and return within a week.

"One of these days you're going to learn there isn't an opportune time to take a vacation when you own your own business," John calmly informed her. "Besides, you are the one who said Ben Atkins was capable of handling things while you're gone."

"He is." It was a rather grudging admission. "But I've worked hard to build the company to its present status. I'm not sure it's wise to leave now when we're launching a critical phase of new advertising. You were the one who advised against selling the company after Mac's death, and encouraged me to operate it myself. Now I'm going to be gone at a time when fast decisions need to be made.''

"And if something important arises, Ben can contact the ship by radio. You aren't going to be completely out of touch," he reminded, countering her argument with calm logic.

"No, I suppose not," Rachel acknowledged and sipped thoughtfully through the straw, coral-red lipstick leaving its imprint on the clear plastic.

"When was the last time you took a vacation?" John changed his tactics, challenging her with the question.

"Five years ago," she admitted, "when Mac and I went fishing in British Columbia."

"You need this vacation," he asserted. "There was a time, shortly after Mac's death, when working long and hard had a therapeutic value, but you're over that stage now. You need to stop working so hard and start enjoying life again.''

"I enjoy my life,'' Rachel insisted, but she knew she was beginning to feel the strain of the constant pressure. It was a long time since she had truly relaxed and taken it easy. This cruise would provide her with a much needed respite from meetings and telephones and paperwork. By the same token she was daunted by the prospect of doing nothing for seven days. "I admit I need to get away and relax for a while, but I don't know what I'm going to do with myself for all that time. It isn't as if I know anybody on board. They're total strangers.''

"Strangers are what you need right now,'' John said wisely. "If you were surrounded by friends, you'd start talking about the business. Instead of leaving it behind, you'd be bringing it with you. Getting to know new people will be good for you. Besides, after working so hard, it's time you were pampered. And a sea cruise is just the place for it. If you don't believe me, ask Fan.''

"These cruise ships treat you like a queen.'' His wife was quick to back up his assertion.

"I never had to lift a hand to do anything when John and I went on that trip through the Caribbean last fall. After taking care of four children and a husband, believe me, that was heaven!"

"I'm sure it's very nice." Rachel didn't question that.

"And the food aboard—it's an epicurean delight," Fan declared. "Of course, it isn't so delightful when you have to lose the five pounds you gained during the cruise."

"All your arguments are very sound," Rachel said, because the pair seemed to be ganging up on her. "But I just have some misgivings about this trip. That doesn't mean I'm not going. I'm here and I have my ticket."

"Then stop saying things that make it sound like you're trying to back out at the last minute," Fan reproved her. "Especially after all I went through last week to make certain you had your ticket. Speaking of that"—a frown flickered across her expression as Fan was distracted by the run of her own thoughts—"I wonder what happened to the ticket they supposedly mailed to you. It's strange you never received it."

"It isn't so strange," John disagreed. "Considering how undependable the mail service is these days, it was probably lost."

"It was sent to the wrong address," Rachel said.

"How do you know that?" Fan looked at her with a frowning interest.

"I meant to tell you about it before, but with all the last-minute packing and preparations, I simply forgot to mention it." She began her answer with an explanation of why she hadn't cleared up the mystery before. "When the cruise line reissued the ticket, it was made out to Mrs. Gardner MacKinley all right, but the address they listed wasn't mine. Obviously the original one was mailed to that address, which is why I never received it."

"That explains it." John shrugged diffidently. "Sooner or later the missing ticket will be returned to the ship line."

"Do you suppose I should contact the Princess Cruises and tell them they have the wrong address listed for Rachel?" Fan asked, ever one to have things neatly in order.

"It's hardly necessary since I have my ticket and my pass to get on board." Rachel didn't see the need for it.

There was a lull in the conversation and Rachel sipped at her drink. A car pulled up to the curb to unload its occupants. Three young couples piled out, dragging with them a cooler and a large tray mounded with assorted sandwiches and cheeses—refreshments for their own private bon voyage party. As the luggage was unloaded from the trunk and given to a waiting baggage handler with a cart, it became apparent that only one couple in the group was going on the cruise. The other four had come along to see them off and tour the ship.

When the car had been emptied, the driver slipped behind the wheel to park it in the lot adjacent to the port terminal while the remaining five waited in front of the terminal entrance. A sleek black limousine swung quietly into the curb-side spot the car had vacated and came to a halt. There was an immediate stirring of interest all around.

Fan leaned closer, murmuring to Rachel, "Who do you suppose is arriving?"

An answer wasn't expected for her question, but Rachel's curiosity was naturally aroused, like everyone else's. The limousine's smoked glass was designed to protect the privacy of the passenger, but it also heightened the interest of those wondering who might be inside.

The·trunk latch was remotely released by a panel button. A second later a uniformed chauffeur was stepping out of the limousine and walking around the hood to open the rear passenger door. All eyes focused on the opening, including Rachel's.

A man emerged, unfolding his long length with loose-limbed ease. Tall, easily over six feet when he finally straightened to his full height, he was well built, wide shouldered, and slim hipped. A breeze immediately rumpled his hair as if it couldn't wait to run its fingers through the virile thickness and feel its vital texture. The slanting rays of an afternoon sun caught the desert-tan highlights that streaked his dark hair. His sun-browned features were strong and handsome, ingrained with a maturity tinged with wry cynicism.

As she studied him Rachel was reminded of a statue she'd seen once. Not because of his trimly muscled build or his male good looks. It was another quality that brought the memory to mind—a tempered hardness of form and character. Yet even that impression seemed belied by the laziness of his stance, so relaxed and at ease.

Rachel guessed he knew he was the cynosure of all eyes, but he appeared indifferent to the attention he attracted. His indifference did not appear to be arrogance, but as if he felt his presence was unimportant.

A slow smile pulled his lips apart, briefly showing a row of white, even teeth. He said something to the chauffeur, the words inaudible, but the soft timbre of his voice drifted to her, husky and warm. The uniformed driver immediately smiled back. Rachel had the feeling it was the natural response of anyone who was the recipient of that smile.

Her gaze traveled with the chauffeur as he moved to the rear of the vehicle and began to unload the luggage from the carpet-lined trunk and pass it to the baggage handler. Then her glance swung back to the man in the tan sports jacket and brown slacks. In the brief interim he had squared around, providing her with a better view of his face.

Experience had hammered out any softness in his strongly handsome features and etched into them an understated virility that didn't rely on good looks for its attraction. A cigarette dangled from his mouth as he bent his head to the match flame cupped in his hand.

The unhurried action served as a misdirection while his partially lidded gaze made a slow sweep of the people on the walk outside. It paused to linger on Rachel with mild interest. There was a deliberateness about him, making no apologies for the good, long look he was taking. She had the sensation that his mind was absorbing her image, measuring her attributes against other women he'd known, but offering no judgment. She stiffened slightly, disturbed in some small way she couldn't define.

A pulsebeat later his gaze moved on as casually as it had paused. The match flame was shaken out while he exhaled the smoke he had dragged from the burning cigarette.

Fan's blonde head changed its angle, tipping a degree toward Rachel. "I don't know who he is," she murmured in an aside, "but he's one hunk of a man."

Silently Rachel agreed with that assessment of the man's potently attractive male looks. There seemed to be some magnetic pull that kept her gaze riveted to him even when she felt that her staring was bordering on rudeness.

Again that lazy smile spread across his face as he shook hands with the chauffeur, taking his leave of the man. A hint of it remained when he turned to the baggage handler and discreetly passed the man a folded bill with the ease of one accustomed to tipping. Then his easy-flowing stride was carrying him to the entrance of the terminal building. As Rachel followed him her gaze encountered John Kemper's frowning expression.

"His face is familiar," John said with a puzzled shake of his head. "But I can't think why I should know him."

"It's obvious he's going on the cruise," Fan said and slowly turned her head to look at Rachel. A light of scheming speculation gleamed in her eyes. "He's just the kind of man you need to meet."

"Fan, don't be silly," Rachel protested, her lips lying together in a patiently amused line.

"I'm serious," her friend insisted.

"Well, I'm not interested in getting involved with any man," Rachel asserted when she realized Fan wasn't teasing. "I'm going on this cruise to relax. I have no intention of being caught up in some shipboard affair."

"Who said anything about getting involved?" Fan lifted upturned palms in a blameless gesture. "But you are traveling on the *Love Boat*."

"Don't remind me." Rachel sighed with mild exasperation at the reference to the long-running television series, which had filmed its location shots aboard the *Pacific Princess*.

"Someone needs to remind you if you haven't thought about it." Fan's look was faintly skeptical.

"Let's just say that I haven't given it *much* thought," she replied. "And if I take any moonlight strolls around the deck, it will probably be alone. There's no percentage in becoming romantically entangled with a stranger for a week.''

''I'm not suggesting romance,'' Fan corrected that impression.

''Then what are you suggesting?'' Rachel demanded, becoming a little impatient with the subject.

Instead of immediately answering her, Fan threw a glance at her husband. ''John, close your ears. A husband shouldn't hear the advice his wife gives to single women.''

An indulgently amused smile twitched the corners of his mouth. ''I'm as deaf as a mouse in a bell tower,'' he promised and looked in another direction, pretending an interest elsewhere.

Fan turned back to Rachel. ''What I'm talking about is something a little more basic than romance,'' she said. ''What you really need is a little sex; something to start the fires burning again. And that man looks like he's got what it takes to deliver the goods.''

Advice like that had been offered before, but it was usually given by the man interested in becoming her sexual partner. If anyone else but her best friend had said that to her, Rachel would probably have thrown the orange drink in their face. Instead she set the container on the ledge and stiffly stood up, waiting as Fan rose also.

"My fires are burning nicely." At the moment most of the inner heat came from suppressed anger. She had never considered herself to be a prude. Lonely though she sometimes was, Rachel hadn't become so desperate for love that she resorted to casual sex.

Struggling against her rising agitation, she turned a cold shoulder to Fan. Her forward-facing gaze looked into the glass front of the terminal building. The shaded interior produced a mirrorlike backing for the glass, causing it to reflect a faint image of her own white-suited figure and obscuring the building's many occupants but not to the extent that she failed to recognize the tall, broad-shouldered man talking to one of the cruise staff.

The sight of him, posed so nonchalantly with one hand casually thrust in the side pocket of his slacks, seemed to add to the seething fury that heated her blood. Unques-

tionably he was sexy but not in any overt kind
of way. It was much more subtle than that.
Rachel recognized that and was impatient
with herself because she did.

While she unwillingly watched him, he was
taken over and introduced to another staff
member, who greeted him familiarly. Then he
was personally escorted past the roped-off
boarding area around the open doorway. Her
last glimpse of him was his tapering silhouette outlined briefly in the rectangular patch
of light marking the doorway. While all the
other passengers had to wait until the ap-
pointed boarding time, he was being escorted
onto the ship. She supposed it meant he had
friends in high places.

"I know I probably sounded crude," Fan
continued, slightly defensive and apologetic.
"But it seems to me that the longer you ab-
stain from taking a lover, the more difficult it
becomes. Rather like losing your virginity all
over."

"Let's just forget it." Severely controlling
her voice, Rachel was aware that her friend's
advice was well intentioned. She was just personally uncomfortable with it.

There was a stirring of activity inside the terminal building. The crowd was beginning to bunch closer together and press forward against the ropes. It appeared that the boarding process would commençe shortly.

Afraid that if she stayed Fan would continue on the same subject, Rachel decided that it would be better if she joined the other passengers inside before she lost her temper. She didn't want to start out on this vacation arguing with her best friend. And somewhere she seemed to have lost her sense of humor. She couldn't turn aside the conversation with a joke that would make light of it, even though she knew it was the best and most diplomatic way to handle it.

"They've started boarding," she said. "They aren't admitting visitors until all the passengers are on the ship, so you two might as well wait here. I'll meet you later on the ship—by the gangway."

"We'll be there." John patted his breast pocket, where he had put their visitor passes.

With that agreement voiced, Rachel left them and walked briefly to the entrance, her white reflection in the glass following and merging as she passed through the open doors. It would be a slow process to board the hundreds of waiting passengers, but this was one time when Rachel didn't mind the long wait in line. It would give her a chance to simmer down. At the moment she was too tense, her nerves strung out like high-tension wires.

Voices ran together, creating a low din as Rachel reduced her pace and approached the pressing crowd of passengers. She found a place in the main flow and let it sweep her along to the gate that funneled them into a single line to the door.

CHAPTER TWO

SHINING PRISTINE white, the ship loomed beside the terminal building, tied to the pier only a few feet from the building's outside walls. Its massive size and sleek, pure lines demanded attention as Rachel followed the slow-moving string of passengers traveling along the raised walk to the gangway.

On the bow of the ship, high blue letters spelled out her name—*Pacific Princess*. The blue and green emblem of the cruise line, a maiden's head with long hair streaming out in waves, was painted on the black-ringed smokestack. Rows of portholes and deck railings marked off her many levels. Rachel was slightly awed by her size and stately majesty.

Ahead photographers were snapping pictures of passengers next to signboards welcoming them aboard the *Pacific Princess*.

Usually they took photos of a couple; sometimes two couples wanted their picture taken together; sometimes it was a family shot.

But Rachel was traveling alone. It was the first time she'd gone on a pleasure trip without Mac or some member of her family or even a friend. The point was brought home to her as she stepped forward to take her turn in front of the camera. She thought she had become used to her solitary state, but she felt awkward and self-conscious. It was an unexpected reaction to something she thought she had accepted.

''How about a big smile?'' the photographer coaxed with the camera to his face so his eye could frame her in the lens.

Rachel tried to oblige, but the forced movement was stiff and strained. The click of the camera captured it on film. Then the photographer was nodding to her that it was over, smiling at her with a hint in his glance of male appreciation for her striking looks.

An absent smile touched the corners of her mouth in return, but it faded quickly on an inner sigh as she stepped forward to make room for the couple behind her. She blamed her raw sensitivity on the strain of overwork and quickened her steps to close on the line of passengers progressing slowly up the gangway. After a couple of days rest she'd be her old self again.

Members of the ship's crew were on hand to receive the boarding passengers and direct them to their assigned staterooms. Rachel walked onto the rich blue carpet of the foyer and paused beside the white-uniformed officer, who inclined his head in greeting to her.

"Welcome aboard the *Pacific Princess*. Your cabin, madam?" His voice carried a British accent, reminding Rachel that the ship was of British registry.

"Mrs. MacKinley. Promenade 347." She had the number memorized after writing it so many times on her luggage tags.

He turned to a young, blond-haired man in a steward's uniform and motioned him forward. "Promenade 347," he repeated to the steward, then turned to Rachel, smiling warmly. "Hanson will guide you to your stateroom suite, Mrs. MacKinley."

"Thank you." Her mouth curved in an automatic response, then Rachel moved past him to follow the young steward across the wide foyer to the stairwell flanked by elevators.

The decision to reserve a suite instead of a simple stateroom had been an impulsive one and admittedly extravagant, since she was traveling alone. Part of it had been prompted by Fan's urging that Rachel should do this vacation up right and travel in style, and part of it had been motivated by a desire to have uncramped quarters where she could lounge in comfortable privacy.

A landing divided the stairs halfway between each deck and split it into flanking arms that turned back on itself to rise to the next deck. The landings, the turns, the lookalike foyers on each deck, began to confuse Rachel as she followed the steward. Already cognizant of the size of the ship, she quickly realized that it would be easy to become turned around with so many decks and the maze of passageways.

Instead of relying solely on her guide, Rachel began to look for identifying signs so she would learn her route to the stateroom and not become lost when she had to find it again.

The striding steward didn't give her much time to dawdle and still keep him in sight.

When they stopped climbing stairs, the steward crossed the foyer and started down a long passageway. The level was identified as the Promenade Deck. Rachel stopped for a second to read the small sign indicating the range of cabin numbers located in the direction of its pointing arrow.

Her gaze was still clinging to the sign when she hurriedly started forward to catch up with the steward before she lost track of him. She didn't see the person approaching from the opposite direction until the very last second. Rachel tried to stop abruptly and avoid the collision, but she had been hurrying too fast to completely succeed.

Her forward impetus almost carried her headlong into the man. She cringed slightly in anticipation of the impact, but a pair of hands caught her by the arms and reduced the collision to a mere bump. She'd been holding her breath and now released it in a rushed apology.

"I'm sorry." Her head came back to lift her gaze upward.

A half-formed smile ·of vague embarrassment froze on her face as Rachel recognized the man from the limousine. Only now his face was mere inches from hers. The detail of his solid features was before her—the sun wrinkles at the corners of his eyes, the angled plane of his jaw and chin, and the smooth, well-defined strength of his mouth.

Her pulse rate shot up as her glance flicked to his lazy brown eyes. A smiling knowledge seemed to perpetually lurk behind their dry brown surfaces. She felt it licking over her as his gaze absorbed her features from the tip of her nose to the curved bow of her lips and the midnight blackness of her hair, then finally to the silver brilliance of her widened gray eyes.

This flash of mutual recognition and close assessment lasted mere seconds. On the heels of it came the recollection of Fan's advice concerning this very man whose hands were steadying her. Rachel went hot at the memory, her glance falling before his as if she thought he might be able to read her thoughts. She began to feel very stiff and awkward.

His hands loosened their hold on her arms and came away. Belatedly Rachel noticed that he was holding his tan jacket, which he swung over his white-shirted shoulder, casually hooking it on a forefinger. His shirt collar was open, exposing the tanned column of his throat.

"I'm sorry," she said stiffly, repeating her apology for bumping into him, trying to distract her thoughts from the tingling sensation on her arms where his hands had been. "I'm afraid I wasn't looking where I was going."

There was a lazy glitter in his eyes as his mouth quirked. "That was my good fortune."

She didn't want him to come back with a remark like that, not with echoes of Fan's advice ringing in her ears. It only added to her discomfort in the whole situation. Unable to respond to the casual advice, Rachel chose to ignore it.

"Excuse me." Her young guide had long since disappeared down the passageway. She brushed hurriedly past the man and started down the corridor in the direction the steward had taken.

It seemed crazy, but she could feel his gaze watching her go. She even knew the moment he turned and continued on his way. Only then did some of the stiffness leave her, the tension easing in her nerves. Slowing her steps slightly, Rachel drew in a deep, calming breath and felt her pulse settling down.

At the aft end of the passageway there was another foyer with its own stairwell and elevators. It was almost an exact duplicate of the one at the forward end of the Promenade Deck. She halted, looking around for some sign to point her in the right direction. Just then the steward appeared, having retraced his steps to look for her.

"Sorry, ma'am." There was a look of chagrin on his young face. "I thought you were right behind me."

"It's all right," she assured him. It didn't seem necessary to explain why she had been detained.

"Your suite is this way."

This time he made sure she stayed at his side as he led the way past the elevator and down a galleria-type corridor to the next section of staterooms. He stopped at the first door on Rachel's left, opened it, then stepped aside so she could enter.

"If there's anything you need, press the button on the telephone," he said. "That will summon your room steward. There's someone on duty twenty-four hours."

"Thank you," Rachel nodded.

"I hope you enjoy your cruise," he said and left her to explore the suite on her own.

Rachel closed the door and turned to survey the large sitting room. The drapes were open, letting in the afternoon light. The room was a blend of warm coral colors with brown upholstered chairs for accent. In addition there was a table and four chairs so she could eat in her room if she preferred. A wet bar stood against one wall, fully stocked with glasses.

The bedroom was tucked in an alcove off the sitting room. The twin beds were built-in and covered with a coral patterned spread. Floor-to-ceiling curtains could be drawn to shut off the bedroom from the sitting area. Rachel inspected the available storage, opening drawers and doors.

Her three pieces of luggage sat on the floor by the bed. For the time being she stowed them in a closet. There would be time enough to unpack later in the evening. At the moment she was only interested in getting it out of the way.

There was a private bath as well, with a huge tub and shower combination, and a well-lighted mirror at the sink vanity. Her quarters were very definitely more than comfortable.

When she returned to the sitting room Rachel spied a cabin key lying on the table and slipped it into her purse. There was a copy of the ship's daily activity paper, the *Princess Patter,* beside it. Rachel glanced through its information section and the schedule of the day's events. There was another small card on the table that gave her the number of her assigned table in the dining room. She noticed that she was in the "late-sitting" group.

With Fan and John Kemper due to come aboard anytime, Rachel didn't think she should linger any longer in her room. She double-checked to be sure she had the key before she left the cabin and retraced her route to the lobby at the gangway.

ALL TOO soon, it seemed, the last call requesting all visitors ashore had sounded and

Rachel was leaning on the railing on the port side of the Promenade Deck and waving to her friends on the pier below. Passengers were lined up and down the railing on either side of her. Some, like herself, had friends or relatives in the crowd on the wharf while others merely wanted to watch the procedures of the ship leaving port.

A few colored paper streamers were prematurely unfurled and tossed to those ashore. The curling ribbons of paper drifted downward. Rachel had a half dozen of the coiled streamers in her hand, presented to her by Fan Kemper for the occasion.

"They're hauling in the lines," someone down the line remarked.

Within minutes the ship began to maneuver away from the pier. The water churned below as the midship engines pushed it away. There was a cheering of voices, and Rachel threw her streamers into the air to join the cascade of bright paper ribbons onto the crowd waving a last good-bye.

As the ship sailed stately away from its port, Rachel lingered with the other passengers. The growing distance between the ship and the pier blurred the faces of the people ashore until Rachel could no longer distinguish her friends from the crowd. On either side of her people began to drift away from the railing. The sun was on the verge of setting, a gloaming settling over the sky.

An evening breeze swept off the water and whipped at her hair before racing on. Rachel lifted her hand and pushed the disturbed strands back into place. A faint sigh slipped from her as she turned from the railing to go back inside.

Her sliding gaze encountered a familiar figure standing at a distance. It was that man again, talking with one of the ship's officers. Irritation thinned the line of her mouth as her glance lingered an instant on the burnished gold lights the sun trapped in his chestnut-dark hair. Of the six hundred plus passengers on the ship it seemed incredible that she should be constantly running into this one person.

Before he had the opportunity to notice her, Rachel walked briskly to the double doors leading inside. Instead of going to her cabin, she descended the stairs to the Purser's Lobby on Fiesta Deck. There were some inquiries she wanted to make about the ship's services, including the procedure for making radio-telephone calls.

Judging by the line at the purser's desk, it seemed there were a lot of other passengers seeking information about one thing or another. There was another line on the mezzanine above her, passengers seeking table assignments or wishing to change the one they had been given. A small group of people were clustered around the board set up in the lobby with a list of all the passengers on board and their cabin numbers.

The congestion was further increased by passengers taking pictures of each other posing on the winding staircase that curved to the mezzanine on the deck above. Rachel decided against joining the line at the purser's counter and entered the duty-free gift shop to browse until some of the crowd cleared.

Half an hour later she realized there was little hope of that. There seemed to be just as many people now as before. Giving up until tomorrow, Rachel started for her stateroom by way of the aft staircase.

The Promenade Deck was three flights up. By the time she reached it, she felt slightly winded. Another couple were on their way down as she took the last step and released a tired breath. The pair looked at her and smiled in sympathetic understanding.

"I'm out of condition," Rachel admitted; she wasn't used to climbing stairs.

"You can always use the elevators," the man reminded her.

"I could, but I need the exercise," she replied.

"Don't we all." His wife laughed.

It was a friendly moment between strangers. When it was over and Rachel was walking down the passageway to her stateroom, there was a hint of a smile on her face. Being on the cruise gave everyone something they had in common and provided a meeting ground to exchange impressions and discoveries.

In this quiet and contemplative mood Rachel entered her stateroom and shut the door. She deposited her purse on the seat cushion of a chair near the door and slipped out of the white jacket, absently draping it over the same chair.

A footfall came from the bedroom. Rachel swung toward the sound, startled. Her mouth opened in shock when the man from the limousine came around the opened curtains. He was busy pushing up the knot of his tie and didn't see her until he lifted his chin to square the knot with his collar. There was an instant's pause that halted his action in mid-motion when he noticed her with a brief flare of recognition in his look.

He recovered with hardly a break in his stride. His glance left her and ran sideways to the wet bar, where a miniature bucket of ice now sat. A faintly bemused smile touched his mouth as he turned to it.

"I asked the room steward to bring me some ice." His lazy voice rolled out the statement. "But I didn't know I was going to be supplied with a companion as well." His sidelong glance traveled her length in an admiring fashion. "I must say I applaud his choice."

Rachel was stunned by the way he acted as if he belonged there. It was this sudden swell of indignation that brought back her voice.

"What are you doing here?" she demanded, quivering with the beginnings of outrage. Her fingers curled into her palms, clenching into rigid fists at her sides.

Nonchalantly he dropped ice cubes into a glass and poured a measure of scotch over them. "I was about to ask you the same question." He added a splash of soda and swirled the glass to stir it.

"I'll have you know this is my cabin. And since I didn't invite you in here, I suggest you leave," Rachel ordered.

"I think you have things turned around." He faced her, a faint smile dimpling the corners of his mouth as he eyed her with a bemused light. "This is my cabin. I specifically requested it when I made my reservations."

"That's impossible!" she snapped. "This is my cabin." To prove it, Rachel turned and picked up her purse. She removed her cruise packet and opened it so he could see that she had been assigned to this stateroom.

He crossed the room to stand in front of her and paused to look at the ticket she held. His brown eyes narrowed slightly and flicked to her, a tiny puzzled light gleaming behind their sharply curious study.

"Is this some kind of a joke?" He motioned to the ticket with his drink. "Did Hank put you up to this?'

"A joke?" Rachel frowned impatiently. "I don't know what you're talking about."

"The name on that ticket," he replied and sipped at his drink, looking at her over the rim. There was a delving quality about his look that seemed to probe into sensitive areas.

Rachel felt a prickling along her defenses. She glanced at the ticket, then back to him. "It's my name—Mrs. Gardner MacKinley. I don't see anything funny about that," she retorted stiffly.

"Since I seem to be suffering from a memory blank, maybe you wouldn't mind telling me just when we were supposed to have been married," he challenged with a mocking slant to his mouth.

For a second she was too stunned to say anything. "I'm not married to you." She finally breathed out the shocked denial.

"At least we agree on that point." He lifted his glass in a mock salute and took another swallow from it.

"Whatever gave you the idea we were?" She stared at him, caught between anger and confusion.

He leaned a hand against the wall near her head, the action bringing him closer to her. There was a tightening of her throat muscles as she became conscious of his physical presence. There was a heightened awareness of her senses that noted the hard smoothness of his cheek and jaw and the crisply fragrant scent of after-shave lotion. The vein in her neck began to throb in agitation.

"The name and address on that ticket—" His glance slid to it again, then swung back to her face, closely watching each nuance in her expression. "If you leave off the Mrs. part, it's mine."

It took a second for the implication of his words to sink in. "Yours?" Rachel repeated. "Do you mean your name is—" She couldn't say it because it was too incredible to be believed.

"Gardner MacKinley," he confirmed with a slight nod of his head. "My friends call me Gard."

Rachel sagged against the wall, all the anger and outrage at finding him in her cabin suddenly rushing out of her. It seemed impossible and totally improbable, yet—her thoughts raced wildly, searching for a plausible explanation. Her glance fell on the ticket.

"The address—it's yours?" She lifted her gaze to his face, seeking confirmation of the claim he'd made earlier.

"Yes." He watched her, as if absorbed by the changing emotions flitting across her face.

"That must be how it happened," Rachel murmured absently.

"How what happened?" Gard MacKinley questioned, tipping his head to the side.

"Last week my friend went to the offices of the cruise line to find out why I hadn't received my ticket. They assured her it had been mailed, but I'd never gotten it. They reissued this one," she explained as the pieces of the puzzle began to fall into place. "I noticed the address was wrong, but I just thought that was why I hadn't received the first one. But it was sent to you," she realized.

"Evidently that's the way it happened," he agreed and finished the rest of his drink.

"It sounds so incredible." Rachel still found it hard to believe that something like this could happen.

"Let's just say it's highly coincidental," Gard suggested. "After all, telephone directories are full of people with the same names. Imagine what it would be like if your surname were Smith, Jones, or Johnson?"

"I suppose that's true," she admitted because he made it seem more plausible.

For a moment he studied the ice cubes melting in his glass, then glanced at her. "Where's your husband?"

Even after all this time the words didn't come easily to her. "I'm a widow," Rachel informed him, all her defenses going up again as she eyed him with a degree of wariness against the expected advance.

But there was no change in his expression, no sudden darkening of sexual interest. There remained that hint of warmth shining through the brown surfaces of his eyes.

"You must have a name other than Mrs. Gardner MacKinley, or is your first name Gardner?" There was a suggestion of a smile about his mouth.

"No, it's Rachel," she told him, oddly disturbed by him even though there had been no overt change in his attitude toward her. When he straightened and walked away from her to the wet bar, she was surprised.

"The foul-up must have happened when our two reservations were punched into the computer." He swung the conversation away from the personal line it had taken and brought it back to its original course. "No one told it differently so it linked the two of us together." His dark gaze ran back to her, alive with humor as his mouth slanted dryly. "What the computer has joined together, let no man put asunder."

His paraphrase of a portion of the marriage ceremony seemed to charge the air with a sudden, intimate tension. There was a knotting in the pit of her stomach, a tightness that came from some hidden source. The

suggestion that this inadvertent union was in
any way permanent sent her pulse to racing.
It was a ludicrous thought, but that certainly
didn't explain this sudden stimulation of all
her senses.

CHAPTER THREE

RACHEL STRAIGHTENED from the wall she had so recently leaned against and broke eye contact with him, but that didn't stop the nervous churnings inside. Moving briskly, she returned the ticket packet to her purse, a certain stiltedness in her actions.

"That's very amusing, Mr. MacKinley." But there was no humor in her voice. Just saying his name and knowing it was the same as her own seemed to add to this crazy turmoil.

"Gard," he insisted, irritating her further with his easy smile because it had a certain directness to it.

She ignored his invitation to address him more familiarly. "We were both assigned to the same cabin by mistake, but it's a mistake that can be remedied," she informed him with a trace of curtness, her gray eyes flashing.

"The simplest thing for you to do would be to simply move to another cabin."

"Now, I disagree." There was a negative tip of his head. "The simplest thing would be to let the present arrangement stand. This suite comes with two *separate* beds, and there's more than enough room for both of us." The corners of his mouth deepened in the suggestion of a dryly amused smile.

All sorts of images flashed through her mind—the prospect of lying in one twin bed knowing he was in the other, bathing with him in the next room, wakening in the morning as he was dressing. Rachel was disturbed by the direction of her own imagination.

It made her rejection that much stronger. "I think not."

"Why?" Behind the calmness of his question she could see that he was amused by her curt dismissal of the idea. "It could be interesting."

"I don't think that is the word I would use to describe it," she replied stiffly. "But it hardly matters, since I have no intention of sharing my cabin with you."

"Somehow I knew that would be your answer," Gard murmured dryly and set his empty glass down to walk to the telephone. She watched him pick up the receiver and dial a number. "This is MacKinley in 347 on the Promenade Deck," he said into the mouthpiece, sliding a glance at Rachel. "We have a rather awkward situation here. You'd better have the purser come up." The response must have been an affirmative one because a moment later he was ringing off. "Until it's decided whose cabin this will be, may I offer you a drink?" Gard gestured toward the wet bar, offering her its selection.

"No, thank you." The urge was strong to pace the room. The purser couldn't arrive soon enough and rectify this whole mess as far as Rachel was concerned, but she tried to control her impatience.

Gard took a pack of cigarettes out of his pocket, then hesitated. "Cigarette?" He shook one partway out of the pack and offered it to her.

"No, I don't smoke but go right ahead." She motioned for him to smoke if he wished.

He gave her a look of mock reproval. "You don't drink. You don't smoke. You don't share your cabin with strange men. You must lead a very pure . . . and dull life." A wickedly teasing light danced in his eyes.

"So others have informed me," Rachel acknowledged and wondered where her sense of humor had gone. Half the reason Gard MacKinley was making these baiting remarks was because she kept snapping at them. She was handling the situation poorly, and she wasn't too pleased about it.

A silence followed, broken only by the strike of a match and a long breath expelling smoke into the air. The quiet was nearly as unnerving to Rachel as the conversation had been.

Gard seemed to take pity on her and asked a casual question. "Is this your first cruise?"

"Yes." Rachel tried to think of something to add to the answer, but her mind was blank.

"Are you traveling alone or do you have friends aboard?" He filled in the gap she'd left with another question.

"No, I'm alone," she admitted. "I don't know a soul."

"You know me," Gard reminded her.

"Yes, I do—now." She was uncomfortable, but how could she be natural with him when they had met so unnaturally?

The knock at the door startled Rachel even though she'd been listening for it. She pressed a hand to her stomach as if to check its sudden lurch. Before she could move to answer it, Gard was swinging across the room to open the door.

"Hello, Gard. It's damned fine to see you again, boy." The officer greeted him with a hearty welcome, clasping his arm as he shook his hand. "Hank told me you were aboard this trip."

"Come in, Jake." Gard escorted the officer into the sitting room.

He was a short, rounded man with full cheeks and a jovial, beaming smile. When he noticed Rachel in the room, his blue eyes brightened with interest and he removed his hat, tucking it under his arm.

"What seems to be the problem?" he asked, looking from one to the other.

"Both Mr. MacKinley and I have been given this cabin," Rachel explained in an even voice. "But we aren't married."

"Even though the British pride themselves on running a taut ship, I doubt if Jake would be either shocked or surprised by such an announcement," Gard informed her dryly, then glanced at the officer. "I'm sorry, Jake. I didn't introduce you. Meet Mrs. Gardner MacKinley."

"Mrs. MacKinley?" he repeated and frowned as if he were sure he hadn't heard right. "But she just said you weren't married." He pointed a finger at Rachel. "Are you divorced? I don't even recall Hank telling me that you'd ever been married."

"I haven't." Gard assured him on that score. "Rachel and I merely share the same name. Unfortunately she doesn't wish to share the same cabin with me." His amused glance danced over to her.

She reddened slightly but managed to keep her poise. "Evidently Mr. MacKinley and I made our separate reservations at approximately the same time, and someone must have assumed that we were man and wife."

"I see how it could happen, all right." The officer nodded and raised his eyebrows. "Well, this is a bit awkward."

"What other staterooms do you have available?" Gard asked.

"That's the problem," he admitted reluctantly. "There aren't any comparable accommodations available. All the suites are taken, and the deluxe outside rooms. The only thing I have empty are some inside staterooms on Fiesta Deck."

"Is that all?" An eyebrow was lifted on a faintly grim expression.

"That's about it." A light flashed in the man's eyes, a thought occurring to him. "Maybe not." He took back his answer and moved to the telephone. "Let me check something," he said as he dialed a number.

Feeling the tension in the air, Rachel strained to hear his conversation, but his voice was pitched too low for her to pick out the words. With his back turned to them, she couldn't even watch his lips. When the officer hung up the phone and turned around, he was smiling.

"The owner's suite is empty this cruise," he informed them. "It's on the Bridge Deck where the officers are quartered. Under the circumstances I can't offer it to Mrs. Mac-Kinley, since it might not look right to have an attractive and unattached woman staying in their area, but you're welcome to it, Gard."

"I accept. And I'm sure Mrs. MacKinley appreciates your concern for her good reputation," he added with a mocking glance in her direction.

He was making her feel like a prude, which she certainly wasn't. The gray of her eyes became shot with a silvery fire of anger, but Rachel didn't retaliate with any sort of denial. It would only add to his considerable store of ammunition.

"I'll arrange for the room steward to bring your luggage topside to the owner's suite," Jake offered. "In the meantime I'll show you to your quarters."

"It's a good thing I didn't get around to unpacking. My suitcases are sitting in the bedroom." Gard turned and faced her. "It was a pleasure sharing the cabin with you—

for however short a period of time. Maybe we can try it again sometime."

"I'm sure you'd like that." Her smile was tinged with a wide-eyed sweetness. At last she'd found her quick tongue, which could answer back his deliberately teasing remarks.

"I'm sure I would," Gard murmured, a new appreciation of her flashing across his expression along with a hint of curiosity.

With his departure the room suddenly seemed very empty and very large. The sharp tang of his after-shave lotion lingered in the air, tantalizing her nose with its decidedly masculine scent. After his stimulating presence there was a decidedly let-down feeling. Rachel picked up the glass he'd drunk from and carried it into the bathroom, where she dumped the watery ice cubes into the sink and rinsed out the glass.

The piped-in music on the radio speakers was interrupted by a ship announcement. "Dinner is now being served in the Coral Dining Room for late-sitting guests." The words were slowly and carefully enunciated by a man with a heavy Italian accent. *"Buon appetito."* The bell-sweet notes of a chime played out a short melody that accompanied the end of the announcement.

But Rachel had no intention of going to dinner until the steward came for Gard's luggage. She didn't want any of her suitcases being accidentally taken to his cabin and have that mix-up on top of the duplicate cabin assignment.

A few minutes later the steward knocked at the door. Curiosity was in his look, but he never asked anything. As soon as Rachel had supervised the removal of Gard's luggage, she freshened her make-up, brushed her waving black hair, and put the white jacket on.

When she arrived at the dining room on the Coral Deck, the majority of the passengers had already been seated. Tonight they weren't expected to sit at their assigned tables. Since she was arriving late, Rachel requested one of the single tables.

After she'd given the dark-eyed Italian waiter her order, her gaze searched the large dining room, unconsciously looking for Gard. Only when she failed to see a familiar face did she realize she'd been looking for him. She immediately ended the search and concentrated on enjoying the superb meal she was served.

Upon entering the cabin on her return from the dining room, Rachel discovered that the steward had been in the room during her absence. The drapes at the window were pulled against the rising of a morning sun and one of the beds was turned down. There was a copy of the next day's *Princess Patter* on the table with its schedule of events.

Briefly she glanced through it, then walked to the closet to take out her suitcases and begin the tedious business of unpacking. It was late when she finally crawled into bed, much later than she had anticipated retiring on her first night at sea. There was little motion of the ship, the waters smooth and calm.

In the darkness of the cabin her gaze strayed to the twin bed opposite from the one she lay in. Its coral spread was smoothed flatly and precisely over the mattress and pillows. Its emptiness seemed to taunt her. She shut her eyes.

THE FEBRUARY sky was blushed with the color of the late-rising sun as Rachel opened the drapes to let the outside light spill into her cabin. According to her watch, it was a few minutes after seven. It seemed that the habit of rising early was not easy to break even when she could sleep late.

She paused a moment at the window to gaze at the gold reflection of the sunlight on the sea's serene surface, then walked to the closet and began to go over her choices of clothes. Her breakfast sitting wouldn't be until half past eight, but coffee was available on the Sun Deck. Although it would probably be warm later in the day, it would likely be cool outside at this early hour of the morning. Rachel tried to select what to wear with that in mind.

A gentle knock came to her door, just loud enough to be heard and quiet enough not to disturb her if she was still sleeping. Rachel tightened the sash of her ivory silk nightrobe as she went to answer the door. A few minutes earlier she had heard the room steward in the passageway outside her stateroom. She expected to see him when she opened the door.

She certainly didn't expect to see Gard MacKinley lounging indolently in her doorway, a forearm braced nonchalantly against its frame. He was dressed in jogging shorts and shoes, a loose-fitting sweatshirt covering his muscled shoulders and chest. Rachel wasn't prepared for the sight of him—or the sight of his long legs, all hard flesh and corded muscle.

The upward-pulled corners of his mouth hinted at a smile while the warm light in his brown eyes wandered over her. Rachel was immediately conscious of her less than presentable appearance. The static cling of her robe's silk material shaped itself to her body and outlined every curve. Her face had been scrubbed clean of all makeup the night before, and she hadn't even brushed her sleep-rumpled hair, its tousled thickness curling in disorder against her face and neck.

Before she could check the impulse, she lifted a hand and smoothed a part of that tangle, then kept her hand there to grip the back of her neck. The suggestion of a smile on his mouth deepened at her action, a light dancing in his look.

"I wouldn't worry about it," Gard advised her with a lazy intonation of his voice. "You look beautiful."

With that, he straightened, drawing his arm away from the frame and moving forward. Her instinctive response was to move out of his way and maintain a distance between herself and his blatantly male form. Too late, Rachel realized that she should have attempted to close the door to her cabin instead of stepping back to admit him. By then his smooth strides had already carried him past her into the sitting room. It was this lapse on her part that made her face him so stiffly.

"What do you want?" she demanded.

There was an interested and measuring flicker of light in his eyes as he idly scanned her face. He seemed to stand back a little, in that silent way he had of observing people and their reactions.

"I made a mistake yesterday evening when I said I hadn't unpacked," Gard replied evenly. "I'd forgotten that I'd taken out my shaving kit so I could clean up before going to dinner. I didn't discover it until late last night. Somehow"—a hint of a mocking twinkle en-

tered his eyes—"I had the feeling you'd get
the wrong idea if I had come knocking on
your door around midnight."

"You're mistaken about the shaving kit."
Rachel ignored his comments and dealt directly with the issue. "You didn't leave it here.
I unpacked all my things last night and I
didn't find anything of yours while I was
putting mine away."

"You must not have looked everywhere
because I left it in the bathroom." He was
unconvinced by her denial that it wasn't in the
cabin.

"Well, you didn't—" But Rachel didn't
have a chance to continue her assertion because Gard was already walking to the bathroom door. She hurried after him, irritated
that he should take it upon himself to search
for it. "You have no right to go in there."

"I know you won't be shocked if I tell you
that I've probably seen the full range of feminine toiletries in my time," he murmured
dryly and paid no attention to her protests,
walking right into the bathroom.

Rachel stopped outside the door, her fingers gripping the edge of the frame, and

looked in. The bathroom was comfortably spacious, but she still didn't intend to find herself in such close quarters with him.

"You look for yourself," she challenged, since he intended to do just that anyway. "You'll see it's not here."

He cast her a smiling look, then reached down and pulled open a drawer by the sink. It was a drawer she hadn't opened because she hadn't needed the space. When she looked inside, there was a man's brown shaving kit.

"Here it is—just where I left it," he announced, dark brows arching over his amused glance.

"So it is." Rachel was forced to admit it, a resentful gray look in her eyes. "I guess I never looked in that drawer."

"I guess you didn't," Gard agreed smoothly—so smoothly it was almost mocking.

He half turned and leaned a hip against the sink, shifting his weight to one foot. A quiver of vague alarm went through Rachel as she realized that he showed no signs of leaving either her cabin or her bathroom. There was a slow, assessing travel of his gaze over her.

"How long will it take you to dress and fix your hair?" he asked.

"Why?"

"So I'll know what time to meet you top-side for some morning coffee."

"It won't make any difference how long it takes for me to get dressed, since I won't be meeting you for coffee," Rachel replied, stung that he was so positive she would agree.

"Why?" he asked in a reasonable tone.

"It hardly matters." She swung impatiently away from the bathroom door, the silken material of her long robe swishing faintly as she moved to the center of the sitting room. When she heard him following her, Rachel whirled around, the robe swinging to hug her long legs. "Hasn't anyone ever turned down an invitation from you?"

"It's happened," Gard conceded. "But usually they gave a reason if only to be polite. And I just wondered what yours is?"

Her features hardened with iron control. Only her eyes blazed to show the anger within. "Perhaps I'm tired of men assuming that I'm so lonely I'll accept the most casual invitation. Every man I meet immediately assumes that because I'm a widow I'm desperate for male companionship." Her scathing glance raked him, putting him in the same category. "They're positive I'll jump at the chance to share a bed with them—or a cabin—just because they can fill out a pair of pants. According to them, I'm supposed to be frustrated sexually."

It didn't soothe her temper to have him stand there and listen to her tirade so calmly. "Are you?" Gard inquired blandly.

For an instant Rachel was too incensed to speak. The question wasn't worthy of an answer, so she hurled an accusation at him instead. "You're no better than the others! It may come as a shock to you, but I'd like to know something about a man besides the size of his shorts before I'm invited into his bed!"

She was trembling from the force of her anger and the sudden release of so much bitterness that had been bottled up inside. She turned away from him to hide her shaking, not wanting him to mistake it as a sign of weakness.

"What does meeting for coffee have to do with going to bed together?" he wondered.

"Or has your experience with men since your husband died been such that you don't accept any invitations?" There was a slight pause before he asked, "Do you want to be alone for the rest of your life?"

The quiet wording of his question seemed to pierce through the barriers she had erected and exposed the need she'd kept behind it. She wanted to love someone again and share her life with him. She didn't want to keep her feelings locked up inside, never giving them to anyone.

When she swung her gaze to look at him, her gray eyes were stark with longing. She had lived in loneliness for so long that she hadn't noticed when it had stopped being grief. His dark gaze narrowed suddenly, recognizing the emotion in her expression. Rachel turned away before she showed him too much of the ache she was feeling.

"No, I don't want to be alone forever," she admitted in a low voice.

"Then why don't you stop being so sensitive?" Gard suggested.

"I'm not," Rachel flared.

"Yes, you are," he nodded. "Right now you're angry with me. Why? Because I think you are a very attractive woman and I've tried to show you that I'm attracted to you."

"You came for your shaving kit," she reminded him, not liking this personal conversation now that she was becoming the subject of it. "You have it, so why don't you leave?"

She tried to brush past him and walk over to open the door and hurry him out, but he caught at her forearm and stopped her. His firm grip applied enough pressure to turn her toward him.

"I'm not going to apologize because I find you attractive and say things that let you know I'm interested," Gard informed her. "And I'm not going to apologize because I have the normal urge to take you in my arms and kiss you."

She looked at him but said nothing. She could feel the vein throbbing in her neck, its hammering beat betraying how his seductive voice disturbed her. She was conscious of his closeness, the hand that came to rest on the curve of her waist, and the steadiness of his gaze.

"And if the kiss lived up to my expectations, I would probably be tempted to press it further," he admitted calmly. "It's natural. After all, what's wrong with a man wanting to take a woman into his arms and kiss her? For that matter, what's wrong with a woman wanting to kiss a man?"

For the life of her Rachel couldn't think of a thing, especially when she felt his hand sliding smoothly to the back of her waist and drawing her closer. As his head slowly bent toward her, her eyelids became heavy, closing as his face moved nearer.

His mouth was warm on the coolness of her lips, moving curiously over them. Her hands and arms remained at her side, neither coming up to hold or resist. The pressure of his nuzzling mouth was stimulating. Rachel could feel the sensitive skin of her lips clinging to the faint moistness of his mobile mouth.

Behind her outward indifference her senses were tingling to life. Her body had swayed partially against him, letting the solidness of his body provide some of her support. There was a faint flavor of tobacco and nicotine on his lips, and the clean scent of soap drifted from his tanned skin.

There was a roaming pressure along her spine as his hand followed its supple line. It created a pleasant sensation and Rachel leaned more of her weight against him, feeling the outline of his hips and thighs through the thin, clinging material of her robe. The nature of his kiss became more intimate, consuming her lips with a trace of hunger. Within seconds a raw warmth was spreading through her system, stirring up impulses that Rachel preferred to stay dormant.

She lowered her head, breaking away from the sensual kiss and fighting the attack of breathlessness. The minute his arms loosened their hold on her, she stepped away, avoiding his gaze.

It would have been so easy to let his experienced skill carry her away. It was so ironic, Rachel nearly laughed aloud. A little sex was what her friend had recommended. There wasn't any doubt in Rachel's mind that Gard could arouse her physical desire, but she wanted more than that.

"You didn't slap my face," Gard remarked after the silence had stretched for several seconds. "Should I be encouraged by that?"

"Think what you like. You probably will anyway," Rachel replied and finally turned around to look at him, recovering some of her calm. "If you don't mind, I'll ask you to leave now. I'd like to get dressed."

"How about coffee on the Sun Deck?" He repeated the invitation that had started the whole thing.

Her wandering steps had brought her to the table where the telephone sat. Rachel pushed the call button to summon the steward, aware that his gaze sharpened as he observed her action.

"Let's do it some other time, Mr. MacKinley," she suggested, knowing that the indefiniteness of her answer was equal to polite refusal.

"Suit yourself." He shrugged but his narrowed interest never left her.

There was a warning knock before the door was opened by the room steward. Curiosity flared when he saw Gard in the cabin, but he turned respectfully to Rachel. "Did you want something, Mrs. MacKinley?"

"Mr. MacKinley had left his shaving kit here. I thought you might have seen it," she lied about the reason she had called him. "But we found it just this minute. Thank you for coming, though."

"No problem," he assured her. "Is there something else I can do? Perhaps I can bring the two of you coffee?"

"No thanks," Rachel refused and looked pointedly at Gard. "Mr. MacKinley was just leaving."

Lazy understanding was in his looks at the way she had maneuvered him into leaving under the escort of the steward. He inclined his head toward her and moved leisurely to the door the steward was holding open.

CHAPTER FOUR

THERE WAS some morning coolness in the breeze blowing through the opened windows at The Lido on the Sun Deck, but her lavender sweater jacket with its cowled hood provided Rachel with just enough protection that she didn't feel any chill. There was a lot of early risers sitting at the tables and taking advantage of the coffee and continental breakfast being served.

On the Observation Deck above, joggers were tramping around the balcony of the sun dome, pushed open to provide sunshine and fresh air to The Lido. As Rachel waited in the buffet line for her coffee she looked to see if Gard happened to be among the joggers. Not all of them had made a full circle before the people in line ahead of her moved and she followed.

She bypassed the fruit tray of freshly cut pineapples, melons, and papaya and the warming tray of sweet rolls, made fresh daily at the ship's bakery. It all looked tempting, but she intended to breakfast in the dining room, so she kept to her decision to have only coffee.

There was an older couple directly in front of her. When she noticed that they were having difficulty trying to balance their plates and each carry a glass of juice and a cup of coffee as well, Rachel volunteered to carry some of it for them. She was instantly overwhelmed by their rush of gratitude.

"Isn't that thoughtful of her, Poppa," the woman kept exclaiming to her husband as she carefully followed her mate to a table on the sheltered deck by the swimming pool.

"You are a good woman to do this," he insisted to Rachel. "Momma and I don't get around so good—but we still get around. Sometimes it's nice to have help, though."

"Please sit with us," his wife urged as Rachel set their glasses of juice on the table for them. "We appreciate so much how you helped us. If you hadn't, I would have spilled something for sure, then Poppa would have been upset and—''. She waved a wrinkled hand in a gesture that indicated she could have gone on about the troubles that might have occurred. ''How can we thank you?'' she asked instead.

''It was nothing, honestly,'' Rachel insisted, a little embarrassed at the fuss they were making over her. Both hands were holding her coffee cup as she backed away from the table. ''Enjoy your breakfast.''

''Thank you. You are so kind.'' The elderly man beamed gratefully at her.

As Rachel turned to see a quiet place to sit and drink her coffee, she spied Gard just coming off the ladder to the Observation Deck. His sweatshirt was clinging damply to him, a triangular patch of wetness at his chest, and his skin glistened with perspiration. He was walking directly toward her. Rachel stood her ground, determined not to spend her entire cruise trying to avoid him. Even though he looked physically tired, there was a vital, fresh air about him, as if all the fast-running blood in his veins had pumped the cobwebs out of his system. She envied that tired but very alive look.

He slowed to a stop when he reached her, his hands moving up to rest on his hips. "Good morning, Mrs. MacKinley." Amusement laced his warm greeting as he smiled down at her, his eyes skimming over her ebony hair framed by the lavender hood.

"Good morning, Mr. MacKinley," she returned the greeting.

His gaze drifted to her lips, as if seeking traces of the imprint his mouth had made on them. There was something almost physical about his look. Rachel imagined that she could feel the pressure of his kiss again.

"I see you have your morning coffee," Gard observed.

"Yes, I do." She braced herself for his next remark, expecting it to be some reference to his invitation.

"I'll see you later." He started forward, changing his angle slightly to walk by her. "I have to shower and change before breakfast."

For a stunned second she turned to watch him leave. Behind her she heard the elderly couple at the table speaking about them.

"Did you hear that, Poppa?" the woman was saying. "They call each other Mister and Missus."

"The way we used to, eh, Momma."

"He called her Mrs. MacKinley," the woman said again.

"And she called him Mr. MacKinley," the man inserted.

"That's so nice and old-fashioned, isn't it?" the woman prompted.

Suppressing the impulse to walk to their table, Rachel moved in the opposite direction. It hardly mattered that they had the mistaken impression she was married to him. Correcting it might involve a long, detailed explanation and she didn't want to go into it. Besides, what they had overheard had brought back some fond memories of their early married life. They were happy, so why should she spoil it with a lot of explanations that didn't really matter to them.

SHORTLY AFTER late-sitting breakfast was announced, Rachel entered the dining room and was shown to her assigned table. It was located in a far corner of the room, quiet and away from the flow of traffic to the kitchen and the waiter service areas. Two couples were already sitting at the table for eight when Rachel arrived.

An exchange of good mornings was followed by introductions. She was immediately confused as to which woman was Helen and which one was Nanette, and their husbands were named something like John or Frank. Rachel didn't even make an attempt to remember their last names. Since they would be sharing every meal together from now on, she knew she would eventually get the right names with the right faces.

While the waiter poured a cup of coffee for her, Rachel glanced over the breakfast menu. A third couple arrived, a young pair in their twenties, compared to what Rachel judged to be the average age of forty for the other four. After they were seated, there was only one vacant chair—the one beside Rachel.

"I'm Jenny and this is my husband, Don," the girl said. There was a bright-eyed, playful quality about her that seemed to immediately lighten the atmosphere at the table.

Her introduction started the roll call around the table again, ending with Rachel. "I'm Rachel MacKinley." Although the others hadn't, she tacked on her surname. She supposed it was probably a business habit.

The waiter hovered by her chair to take her order. "Orange juice, please," she began. "Some papaya, two basted eggs, and Canadian bacon."

When she partially turned in her chair to pass the menu to the waiter, Rachel saw Gard approaching their table. All the ones close to them were filled, so his destination could be none other than the empty chair next to her.

Something should have forewarned her. Until this moment she hadn't given a thought to where he might be seated. But it was obvious they would be seated at the same table. They had been assigned to the same cabin, so naturally as man and wife, supposedly, they would be assigned to the same table.

That moment of shocked realization flashed in her eyes, and Gard saw the flicker of surprise in their gray depths. A smile played at the edges of his mouth. Rachel faced the table again and reached for her coffee cup, trying to keep the grim resignation out of her expression.

"Sorry I'm late," Gard said to the table in general as he pulled out the vacant chair beside Rachel and sat down. "It took longer to shower and change than I thought. Has everyone ordered?"

"We just got here, too," said Jenny, of the young married couple, assuring him quickly that he wasn't the only late arrival. "I'm Jenny, and this is my husband, Don."

The round-robin of names started again, but Rachel stayed out, not needing to introduce herself to him. "I'm Gard MacKinley," he finished the circle and unfolded the napkin to lay it on his lap. "Is this your first cruise, Jenny?"

"Yes. It's kind of a second honeymoon for Don and me," she explained. So far, Rachel couldn't recall Jenny's young husband saying a word. "Actually I guess it is our first honeymoon since we didn't go anywhere after our wedding. Both of us had to work, so we kept putting it off. Then the baby came—"

"You have a baby?" The balding man looked at her in surprise. Helen's husband— or was it Nanette's? As many times as their names had been said, Rachel would have thought she'd have them straight, but with Gard sitting beside her, she wasn't thinking too clearly.

There was a crisp darkness to his hair, still damp from the shower, and the familiar scent of his after-shave lotion drifted to her. No matter how she tried not to notice, he seemed to fill her side vision.

"You don't look old enough to be a mother," the balding, forty-year-old man insisted as he eyed the young girl.

"Timmy is six years old, so I've been a mother for a while." Jenny laughed. "I'm twenty-five."

"Where's your little boy?" Helen or Nanette asked.

"Grandma and Grandpa are keeping him so Don and I could take this cruise. It was a chance of a lifetime, and we couldn't pass it up. The company Don works for awarded him this all-expense-paid cruise for being the top salesman in his entire region." It was plain to see how proud she was of his achievement. "It's really great, even if I do miss Timmy already."

"Nanette and I have three children," the man said, providing Rachel with the name of his wife.

"We have four." Which meant that woman was Helen. Helen with the henna-hair—Rachel tried for a word association and discovered the woman had turned her glance to her. "How many children do you have?"

"None," she replied, knowing how much she regretted that now. The waiter came and set the orange juice and papaya before her, thus relieving the need to add anything more to her answer.

"You're leaving it a little late, aren't you...Gard?" Helen's husband hesitated before coming up with his name.

"I suppose I am," he murmured dryly and slid a bemused glance at Rachel.

The elderly couple was one thing, but Rachel didn't intend to let this misconception continue. Her cheeks were warm when she looked away from him to face the rest of their companions at the table.

"Excuse me, but we aren't married, even though we do have the same surname." Her assertion attracted startled and curious looks to both of them. "I know it's all very confusing."

"I'm sure you can all appreciate that it's a long and complicated story." Gard quietly followed up on her statement. "So we won't bore you with the details. But she's right. We aren't married to each other."

There was an awkward silence after their announcement. Rachel had the feeling that henna-haired Helen would love to have been "bored with the details." There were a lot of questions in their eyes, but Gard's phrasing had indicated they wouldn't be welcomed. For the time being, their curiosity was being forced to the side.

A minute later everyone was trying to talk at once and cover up that awkward moment. The waiter took the last three breakfast orders while the assistant served the meals to the first ones. With food to be eaten, there wasn't as much need for conversation.

"What kind of work do you do?" Rachel heard someone at the table ask of Gard. It probably seemed a safe inquiry. She slid him a curious, side-long glance, realizing again how little she knew about this man.

"I'm an attorney in Los Angeles," Gard replied.

Rachel had never prided herself on being able to fit people to occupations by sight, yet she wouldn't have guessed he was in the law profession either. There was no resemblance at all between Gard and John Kemper. Thinking of her friend's husband, she was reminded that John thought he had recognized Gard. Since they were in the same profession in the same city, it was probable he had.

"Is this your first cruise?" Jenny put to him the same question he had asked her.

"No." There was a brief show of a smile. "I've sailed on the *Pacific Princess* many times. The engineer happens to be a personal friend of mine. This is about the only way to spend any time with him, since he's out to sea more than he's in port."

Which explained to Rachel why it had appeared he'd been given preferential treatment when he'd been allowed onto the ship prior to the normal boarding time—and why the purser had known him.

The table conversation digressed into a discussion of the crew, the advantages of working aboard ships, and speculation about the length of time they were away from home at any one stretch. Rachel mostly listened while she ate her breakfast.

She stayed at the table long enough to have a last cup of coffee after the meal. When Nanette and her husband pushed back their chairs to leave, she elected to follow them. Gard still had a freshly poured cup of coffee to drink—not that she really thought he would make a point of leaving when she did, or even wished to avoid it. But when she left the dining room, she was alone.

THE SHIP was huge, virtually a floating city with a population of almost a thousand. It was amazing to Rachel how many times she saw Gard that first day at sea, given the size of the ship and the number of people aboard. Some of it was to be expected, since he was assigned to the same station when they had emergency drills that morning. Naturally she saw him at lunch—and again in the after-

noon when she went sunning on the Observation Deck.

Soon she would be meeting him again at
dinner. It was nearly time for the late-sitting
guests to be permitted into the dining room.
In anticipation of that moment a crowd had
begun to gather, filling the small foyer outside the dining room and overflowing onto the
flight of steps. Rachel waited in the stair
overflow, standing close to the bannister.

With the suggested dress that evening calling for formal wear, there was a rainbow of
colors in the foyer. The style of women's dress
seemed to range over everything from simple
cocktail dresses to long evening gowns, while
the men wore dark suits and ties or tuxedos.

Her own choice of dress was a long flowing
gown in a simple chemise style, but the black
tissue faille was a match with her jet-black
hair. A flash of silver boucle beadings and
cording was created by the splintered lightning design across the bodice, a compliment
to her pewter-grey eyes. Rachel had brushed
her black hair away from her face, the curling ends barely touching her shoulder tops.

Her only jewelry was a pair of earrings, dazzling chunks of crystal. The result was a striking contrast between the understatement of the gown's design, with its demure capped sleeves and boat neckline, and the sleek, sexy elegance of black hair and fabric.

Near the base of the stairs Rachel spotted the henna-haired Helen and her husband, Jack, standing next to Nanette and her husband, whose name Rachel still hadn't gotten straight. She considered joining them, since they shared the same table, but it would have meant squeezing a place for herself in the already crowded foyer, so Rachel decided against it.

Her attention lingered on the couples. Helen looked quite resplendent in a red and gold evening dress that alleviated some of the brassiness of her copper-dyed hair. When she turned to say something to Nanette, her voice carried to Rachel.

"I don't care what you say," she was insisting. "No one will be able to convince me those two are brother and sister—or even cousins."

Nanette's reply was lost to Rachel, but she tensed at Helen's remark. Although Helen hadn't identified the people by name, Rachel had an uneasy suspicion she was one of them. A second later it was obliquely confirmed.

"You heard both of them say they weren't married, but they are still sharing the same cabin. I know," Helen stated with a smug little glance. "I was looking at the roster of passengers this afternoon to find out what cabin the Madisons were in so I could call them and change our bridge date. It was right there in black and white—both of their names with the same cabin number. Just what does that suggest to you?"

There was a sinking feeling in the pit of Rachel's stomach. It was obvious that Helen had construed that she and Gard were lovers. It was one thing to have people believe they were married, and another thing entirely to have them suspect they were conducting an illicit affair.

With the way Helen's mind was running now, Rachel doubted that she would ever believe the true story. The coincidence was so improbable that she would think it was a poor attempt to cover up their affair. Trying to explain what had actually happened would be futile now. More subtle tactics were required.

The dining room opened and the waiting guests poured in. Rachel let herself be swept along with the inward flow while her mind continued to search for a way to divert the mounting suspicions. The two couples were already seated when she approached the table.

"That's a stunning gown you're wearing, Rachel," Helen complimented as Rachel sat in the chair the waiter held for her. "Especially with your black hair."

"Thank you." Rachel smiled with poise, not revealing in her expression that she had any knowledge of the conversation she'd overheard. "It was a favorite of my late husband's," she lied, since she had purchased it the year after Mac's death to wear to a social function she had been obliged to attend.

"You're a widow?" Nanette inquired.

"Yes." Rachel didn't have an opportunity to add more than that, the exchange interrupted by Gard's arrival. On its own, it did nothing to dispel suspicion.

Her glance went to him as he pulled out the chair beside her. His black formal suit enhanced the long, lean look of him, adding to that worldly, virile air. The hand-tailored lines of the jacket were smoothly formed to the breadth of his shoulders and his flatly muscled chest. The sight of him made a definite impact on her senses, alerting her to the powerful male attraction that he held.

"Good evening." It was a general greeting in a masculinely husky voice as Gard sat down and brought his chair up to the table. Then he turned a lazy and probing glance to her. She felt the touch of his gaze move admiringly over her smoothly sophisticated attire. "I didn't see you at the captain's cocktail party in the Pacific Lounge."

"I didn't go," she replied evenly, but she had difficulty preventing her breath from shallowing out under his steady regard.

"So I gathered," he murmured dryly, as if mocking her for stating the obvious.

Out of the corner of her eye Rachel was conscious that Helen was interestedly observing their quiet exchange. She increased the volume of her voice slightly, enough to allow Helen to hear what she was saying.

"You never did mention how you liked the owner's suite," she said to Gard. "Is it satisfactory?"

A smile lurked in his dry brown eyes, knowledge showing that he had caught the change in her voice while he attempted to discern the purpose. Rachel tried to make it appear that her inquiry was merely a passing interest, with no ulterior purpose.

"I could hardly find fault with the owner's suite." Gard spoke louder, too. Covertly Rachel stole a look at the red-haired woman and observed the flicker of confusion as it became apparent that they weren't sharing a cabin. "Why don't you come up after dinner and I'll give you a tour of it?" Gard invited smoothly. Rachel shifted her glance back to him.

Any distance she had managed to put between them in Helen's mind, had been wiped out by his few words, which could be read with such heavy suggestion. Irritation glittered as she met his dry glance.

"I hardly think that would look proper, would you?" she refused with mock demureness.

"And we must be proper at all times, mustn't we?" he chided in a drolly amused tone.

His response was even more damning. Seething, Rachel gave up the conversation and reached stiffly for her menu. By innuendo Gard had implied that they were having an affair and trying to cover it up in front of others. At this point an outright denial would add fuel to the growing suspicions, and Rachel didn't intend to feed anything but herself.

The waiter paused beside her chair, pen and pad in hand. Rachel made a quick choice from the menu selection. "Prosciutto ham and melon for an appetizer," she began. "The cold cream of avocado soup and the rainbow trout almondine."

There was a lull in the table talk as the others perused the menu and made their decisions. When the young couple joined them, Rachel deliberately turned away from Gard and engaged the talkative Jenny in conversation.

CHAPTER FIVE

THERE WAS a languid warmth to the night air as the ship's course entered the fringes of the tropics. The breeze was no more than a warm breath against her bare arms as Rachel stood at the railing and looked into the night. A wrap was not necessary in this mild air.

Beyond the ship's lights the sea became an inky black carpet, broken now and then by a foamy whitecap. Far in the distance lights winked on the horizon, indicating land, but there was no visible delineation between where the sea stopped and the land began, and the midnight sky faded into the distant land mass.

The stars were out, a diamond shimmer of varying brilliance, and the roundness of a silver moon dissolved into a misty circle. In the quiet there was only the muted sound of the ship's engines and the subdued rush of water passing the ship's cleaving hull.

She had the port side of the Promenade Deck to herself. The passengers who hadn't retired for the night were either attending one of the lounge shows or gambling at one of the casinos on board. After dinner Rachel had sampled each of the ship's entertainment offerings until a restlessness had taken her outside into the somnolent warmth of the tropical night.

Her mind seemed blank of any thoughts save the gathering of impressions of the night's surroundings. The opening of a door onto the outer deck signaled the intrusion of someone into her solitude. Rachel sighed in a resigned acceptance of the fact. It was too much to expect that it could have stayed this way for long, not with the number of passengers aboard.

With idle interest she glanced back to see her fellow sojourner of the night. Her fingers tensed on the polished wood railing as she saw Gard's dark figure against the lighted backdrop of the ship's white bulkhead. His head was bent, the reflected glow of a cupped match flame throwing its light on the angular planes of his handsome features.

When he straightened and shook out the match, there was no indication that he'd seen her. The blackness of her long gown and hair helped to lose her form in the darkness of the night. Rachel held herself still, yet she was disturbed by the certain knowledge that it was inevitable that he would eventually notice her standing there, off to one side.

She waited and watched while he turned his gaze seaward. As the moment of discovery was prolonged, the anticipation of it began to work on her nerves. Her pulse was jumping when his gaze made an idle drift toward the stern. There was the slightest hesitation before he changed his angle and wandered over to her. Rachel made a determined effort to appear indifferent to his approach, casually turning her gaze away from him to the distant land lights.

"I thought you'd be safely tucked in your bed by now," Gard said, casually voicing his surprise at finding her there.

When he stopped, it was only inches from her—much too close for her strained composure to handle. Rachel turned at right angles to face him, thus increasing the intervening space. She felt the stirring of her senses in direct reaction to his presence.

"It's such a beautiful night that I came out for some fresh air before turning in." It was a defensive answer, as if she needed to justify her reason for being there. She was disturbed by the effect he was having on her.

"Don't let my coming chase you inside," Gard murmured, seeming to know it was in her mind to leave now that he was here.

"I won't," she replied in denial of her true desire.

"It's a calm night," he observed, briefly releasing her from the steadiness of his dark gaze to cast an eye out to sea. "You're lucky to have such smooth seas on your first cruise."

"It's been perfect," Rachel agreed.

His gaze came back to drift over her smoothly composed features. "It isn't always like this when you sail on the 'bosom of the deep.' At times you're forcibly reminded that bosoms have been known to heave and swell."

The downward slide of his gaze lingered on the bodice of her gown, subtly letting her know that he was aware of the agitated movement of her breasts, which betrayed her altered breathing rhythm. The caressing quality of his look seemed to add to the excitement of her senses. Irritated that he had noticed her disturbance and, worse, that he had drawn attention to it, Rachel could barely suppress her resentment.

"And I'm sure you are an expert on bosoms, aren't you, Mr. MacKinley?" There was veiled sarcasm in her accusing observation.

"I'm not without a limited experience on the subject," Gard admitted with a heavy undertone of amusement in his voice.

"I believe that," she said stiffly.

"I knew you would," he murmured and dragged deeply on the cigarette. Smoke clouded the air between them, obscuring Rachel's view of him. "I don't believe I mentioned how becoming that gown is to you."

"Thank you." Rachel didn't want a compliment from him.

"I suppose it's fitting. Black, for a not-so-merry widow." He seemed to taunt her for the apparent absence of a sense of humor.

"It's hardly widow's weeds." She defended her choice of dress. "No well-dressed woman would be without a basic black in her wardrobe."

"I'm glad to hear it. If you aren't regarding that gown as widow's black, you must have begun accepting social invitations," Gard concluded. "I'm having a small cocktail party in my suite tomorrow evening and I'd like you to come."

"A small party...of one?" Rachel was skeptical of the invitation. A jet-black brow arched in challenge. "Am I supposed to accept, then find out when I arrive that nobody else was invited?"

"That's a bit conceited, don't you think?" The glowing red tip of his cigarette was pointed upward for his idle contemplation of the building ash before his glance flicked to her.

"Conceited?" His response threw her.

"You inferred my invitation was a ruse to get you alone in my cabin. That is presuming that I *want* to get you alone in my cabin. Don't you think you're jumping to premature conclusions?''

''I . . .'' Rachel was too flustered to answer, suddenly caught by the thought that she might have misjudged him. An inner heat stained her cheeks with a high color.

An ashtray was attached to the railing post and Gard snubbed out the cigarette and dropped the dead butt into it. When he looked at Rachel, she was still struggling for an answer.

''I admit the idea is not without a definite appeal, but it isn't behind the reason I invited you to my suite,'' he assured her. ''I am having a few of my friends on board in for cocktails—Hank and the purser among others. I thought you might like to join us—especially since you expressed an interest in the suite at dinner this evening.''

''That was for Helen's benefit.'' Rachel admitted the reason behind her inquiry.

''Why?'' he asked with a quizzical look.

''Because she found our names on the passenger list posted in the Purser's Lobby, with the same cabin number.'' She paused to lend emphasis to the last phrase. "She remembered I had said we weren't married. She put two and two together and came up with a wanton answer. So I tried to make it clear to her that we weren't sharing a cabin."

A low chuckle came from his throat, not improving the situation at all. Her brief spate of embarrassment fled, chased by a sudden rush of anger.

"I don't think it's funny," Rachel said thinly.

"It's obvious you don't," Gard controlled his laughter, but it continued to lace through his voice. "It wouldn't be the first time an unmarried couple shared the same cabin on a ship. Why do you care what the woman thinks? You know it isn't true and that should be good enough."

"I knew I shouldn't have expected you to understand." It was a muttered accusal as Rachel made to walk past him rather than waste any more of her time trying to make him see her side of it.

A black-sleeved arm shot out in front of her and blocked the way, catching her by the arm and swinging her back to face him. Both hands held her when she would have twisted away. A slate-colored turbulence darkened her eyes as Rachel glared up at him.

"Why should it upset you so much because a bunch of strangers might think we're having an affair?" There was a narrowed curiosity in his probing look. "I'm beginning to think the lady protests too much," Gard suggested lazily.

"Don't be ridiculous." But Rachel strongly suspected that she had become too sensitive about any involvement with him, thanks to Fan's advice. It had put her thoughts toward him on a sexual basis right from the start.

The grip of his hands was burning into her flesh, spreading the sensation of his touch through her body. In defense of being brought any closer to him, her hands had lifted and braced themselves against the flatness of his hard stomach.

"What is it you're fighting, Rachel?" he asked with a quizzical look. "It isn't me. So it must be yourself."

"I simply find it awkward being alone with you when so many people have made the mistake of thinking we're married," she insisted, her pulse flaring at his contact with him. "It's bound to put ideas in your head."

"And yours?" Gard suggested knowingly.

There was a split-second hesitation before Rachel slowly nodded. "Yes, and mine, too."

"And these ideas," he continued in a conversational tone while his hand began absently rubbing her arms and edging closer to her shoulder blades in back, slowly enclosing the circle, "you don't want anything to come of them."

"Nothing would," she insisted because the cruise only lasted seven days. And at the end of it they would also part. That was always the way of it. These sensations she was feeling now would leave, too, when the freshness of them faded.

"How can you be so sure?" Gard questioned her certainty.

"I'm not a starry-eyed girl anymore." She was a mature woman with certain adult needs that were beginning to be brought home to her as she started to feel the warmth of his body heat through the thin fabric of her gown. "I know all things have a beginning and an end."

"But it's what's in between that counts," he told her and lowered his head to fasten his mouth onto her lips.

The searching intimacy of his kiss unleashed all the restless yearnings to sweep through her veins and heat her with their rawness. Her hands slid inside the warmth of his jacket and around the black satin cummerbund to spread across the corded muscles of his back, glorying in the feel of the hard, vital flesh beneath her fingers.

There was sensual expertise in his easy parting of her lips and the devastating mingling of their mouths. Her senses were aswim with the stimulating scent of him, male and musky. The beat of her heart was a roar in her ears, deafening her to any lingering note of caution. His shaping hands moved at random over her spine and hips, pressing her to his driving length.

A raw shudder went through her as his mouth grazed across her cheek to nibble at her ear, his breath fanning the sensitive opening and sending quivers of excitement over her skin. Rachel turned her head to the side when he continued his intimate trail down the cord in her neck and nuzzled at the point where it joined her shoulder. She could hear the roughened edge of his breathing. There was a measure of satisfaction in knowing she wasn't the only one aroused.

Then he was drawing back slightly to rest his hard cheekbone against her temple, his lips barely brushing the silken texture of her black hair. While his hands were curved to the hollow of her back, Rachel slipped her arms from around him so she could glide them around his neck.

"I told you it's what's in between that counts," Gard said with a rough edge to his voice that left her in no doubt of his desires. "And you can't deny there's something between us."

"No." The way she was trembling inside, Rachel couldn't possibly deny it. Neither could she tell whether it was purely sexual or if there was an emotional fire there as well. Liking a person was often a spontaneous thing; so was physical attraction. But love took a little longer.

"I thought I'd get an argument out of you on that one," he murmured, absently surprised at her easy agreement, but only she knew the qualification she had attached to it.

When his mouth turned toward her, she welcomed its possession. Her fingers curled into the mahogany thickness of his hair to pull his head down and deepen the kiss. She arched her body more tightly against the vital force of his, her breasts making round impressions on his solid chest. There was a completeness to the moment, the iron feel of a man's arms about her and the passion of a hungry kiss breathing life into her desires.

Locked together in the heat of their embrace, it was several seconds before either of them became aware of the suppressed titters behind them and the whispered voices. Their lips broke apart as they both turned their heads to see the elderly couple tiptoeing past them. Rachel recognized them as the pair that had been so grateful for her help that morning when she had carried juice to the table for them.

They had seemed a romantic pair despite their advanced age. She didn't really mind that they had been the ones who had seen her kissing Gard. Still, this was a fairly public place to indulge in such private necking. She lowered her arms to his chest and gently pushed away.

"I think I'd better go to my cabin before I become drunk on all this fresh air," Rachel murmured.

"It wasn't the air I found intoxicating," Gard countered with lazy warmth and let her move out of the circle of his arms.

"I'll bet you've used that line more than once." The lighthearted feeling prompted her to tease him.

"As an attorney, I'd do well to plead the Fifth Amendment rather than respond to that remark," he retorted and held out a hand to her. "I'll walk you to your cabin."

"No." Rachel put her hands behind her back, in a little girl gesture, to hide them from his outstretched palm. "I'll tell you good night here."

There was a hesitation before he surrendered to her wishes. "I'll see you at breakfast in the morning . . . Mrs. MacKinley."

Something in the way he said her name made it different, like it was his name she possessed. Her heart tumbled at the thought, her pulse racing. She schooled her expression to give none of this away to him and smiled instead.

"I'll see you in the morning." She avoided speaking his name and swung away to walk to the steps leading to the door.

After she had pulled it open, she paused and turned to look aft. He was standing at the railing where they had been, lighting another cigarette, all male elegance in his black formal suit. The urge was strong to go back to his side, and Rachel lifted her long skirt to step over the raised threshold and walked inside before that urge could override her sense of caution.

AT BREAKFAST the next morning Gard extended invitations to his private cocktail party to the three couples at their table. After they had accepted, his roguish glance ran sideways to Rachel.

"Will you come now?" His question mocked her with the proof that she wasn't the only one invited, as she had once accused.

"Yes, thank you." She kept her answer simple, knowing how the red-haired woman was hanging on her every word and partly not caring. She'd run into gossips before who simply had to mind everybody's business but their own.

After last night there was no point in denying her attraction to Gard any longer—and certainly not to herself. She had begun to think that if a relationship developed on the cruise, it wouldn't necessarily have to end when the ship reached its destination in Acapulco. Both of them lived in Los Angeles. They could continue to see each other after this was over. Part of her worried that it might be dangerous thinking. But Rachel knew she was nearly ready to take the chance.

After she had finished her morning meal, she stopped in the Purser's Lobby on her way topside to the Sun Deck. For a change no one was waiting at the counter for information. When Rachel asked to speak to the purser, an assistant directed her to his private office.

When she entered, his short, round body bounced off the chair and came around the desk to greet her. "Good morning, Mrs. MacKinley." His recognition of her was instant, accompanied by a jovial smile. "No more mix-ups, I trust."

"Only one," she said, admitting the reason for wanting to see him. "The passenger list posted outside—"

"That oversight has already been corrected," he interrupted her to explain. "I saw Gard early this morning and he mentioned that he was still listed as being in the cabin assigned to you. I changed that straightaway."

"Oh." She hadn't expected that. "I'm sorry. It seems I've taken your time for nothing."

"I wouldn't worry about that," he insisted and walked with her as she turned to leave. "Will I be seeing you at the cocktail party Gard is having tonight?"

"Yes, I'm coming," she nodded.

"We've been giving him a bad time about having a wife on board," he told her with a broad wink. "His friends have had a good laugh over the mix-up, although I know it was probably awkward for you."

"It was, at the time," Rachel admitted, but her attitude had changed since then, probably because her wariness of Gard was not so strong.

"If I can help you again anytime, come see me." When they reached his office door, he stopped. "I'll see you tonight."

"Yes." She smiled and moved away into the lobby.

As Rachel headed for the gracefully curved staircase rising to the mezzanine of Aloha Deck, her course took her past the board with the passenger list. She paused long enough to see for herself that the cabin number beside Gard's name had been changed. It was no longer the same as hers.

It was late in the afternoon when the ship's course brought it close to a land mass. Rachel stood at the railing with the crowd of other passengers and watched as they approached the tip of the Baja Peninsula, Cabo San Lucas.

The cranberry-colored jump-short suit she wore was sleeveless with a stand-up collar veeing to a zippered front. It showed the long, shapely length of her legs and the belted slimness of her waist. Even though her skin was slow to burn in the sun, Rachel had limited her amount of exposure to this hot, tropical sun. As a result her arms and legs had a soft, golden cast.

A brisk breeze was taking some of the heat out of the afternoon. It whipped at her black hair and tugged a few wisps from the constraining ponytail band, blowing them across her face. With an absent brush of her hand she pushed them aside and watched while the ship began its swing around the point of Cabo San Lucas.

Around her the passengers with cameras were snapping pictures of the stunning rock formations. Centuries of erosion by the sea and weather had carved the white rocks, creating towering stacks and spectacular arches to guard the cape. At this point of land, the Sea of Cortez met the waters of the Pacific Ocean.

As the *Pacific Princess* maneuvered into the bay, giving the passengers a closer look at the sprawling village of San Lucas, Rachel was absently conscious of the person on her left shifting position to make room for someone else. Those with cameras were constantly jockeying for a better position at the rail, and the non-photographers among the passengers generously made room for them. So she thought nothing of this movement until she felt a hand move familiarly onto the back of her waist.

Her body tensed, her head turning swiftly. The iciness melted from her gray eyes when she saw Gard edge sideways to the railing beside her. She felt the sudden sweep of warm contentment through her limbs and relaxed back into her leaning position on the rail.

"It's quite a sight, isn't it?" Rachel said, letting her gaze return to the white cliffs and the small village tumbling down the hillside to the bay. Then she remembered that Gard was a veteran of this cruise. "Although you've probably seen it many times before."

"It's still impressive." The soft, husky pitch of his voice seemed to vibrate through her, warm and caressing. "You didn't come down to lunch."

"No," she admitted, conscious of the solid weight of his arm hooked so casually around her waist. "I realized I couldn't keep eating all these wonderful meals. I have to watch my figure," she declared lightly, using the trite phrasing.

When she turned her head to look at him again, her pulse quickened at the way his inspecting gaze slowly traveled down the length of her body as if looking for the evidence of an extra pound or two. Her breasts lifted on an indrawn breath that she suddenly couldn't release. The soft material of her jump-shorts was stretched by the action and pulled tautly over her maturely rounded breasts.

Her stomach muscles tightened as his gaze continued its downward inspection and wandered over the bareness of her thighs. It was more than the mere intimacy latent in his action. He seemed to be taking possession of her, body and soul. Rachel was shaken by the impression. The impact wasn't lessened when his gaze came back to her face and she saw the faintly possessive gleam in the brown depths of his eyes.

"I don't see anything wrong with your figure," he murmured, understating the approval that was so obvious in his look.

Rachel curled her fingers around the railing and tried to keep a hold on reality. "There would be if I started eating three full meals a day." She stuck to the original subject, not letting him sidetrack her into a more intimate discussion.

"You could always come jogging with me in the mornings and run off that extra meal," Gard suggested.

"No thanks," Rachel refused with a faint laugh. "I came on this cruise to rest and relax. I don't plan to do anything more strenuous than—"

"Making love?" he interrupted to finish the sentence with his suggestion.

Everything jammed up in her throat, blocking her voice and her breath and her pulse. Rachel couldn't speak; she couldn't even think. The seductive phrase kept repeating itself in her mind until a resentment finally wedged through her paralyzed silence because he was setting too fast a pace.

"Don't be putting words in my mouth." Rachel faced the village, her features wiped clear of any expression.

"Why not?" He continued to study her profile with lazy keenness. "Last night you admitted you had ideas in your head. What's wrong with saying the words to go along with them?"

The hand on her waist moved in a rubbing caress, its warm pressure seeming to go right through the material to her skin. Rachel felt the curling sensation of desire beginning low in her stomach. A hardened glint came into her gray eyes as she swung her gaze to him.

"Because some ideas are stupid, and I'd rather not turn out to be a fool." It was too soon for her to know whether she could handle a more intimate relationship with him, and she refused to be rushed into a decision.

His faintly narrowed gaze measured her, then a slow smile spread across his face. "I guess I can't argue with that." Gard straightened and let his hand slide from her waist. "Don't forget cocktails at seven thirty in my suite."

There was an instant when Rachel had an impulse to change her mind and not go, even though she wanted to attend the party. It was something she couldn't explain.

"I'll be there." She nodded.

"Good." He glanced at the watch on his wrist, then back at her. "I'll see you in a couple of hours then. In the meantime, I'd better go shower and dress—and make sure there's plenty of mix and snacks on hand.''

"Okay." Rachel didn't suggest that he leave the party preparations until later and stay with her a little longer.

His gaze lingered on her, as if waiting for her to say there was plenty of time. Then he was leaving her and walking away from the railing.

Soberly she watched him striding away, her gaze wandering over the broad set of his shoulders beneath the form-fitting knit shirt. Somehow Rachel had the feeling that Gard was skilled at playing the waiting game. She began to wonder whether he wasn't patiently wearing down her resistance—and an affair was a foregone conclusion.

Troubled by the thought, her eyes darkened somberly as she swung back to the rail. A wrinkled hand patted the forearm she rested on the smooth wood, drawing Rachel's startled glance to the elderly woman beside her. There was no sign of her husband, but Rachel recognized the woman instantly as half of the couple she'd helped the day before.

"Don't be too hard on your husband, Mrs. MacKinley." Her look was filled with sympathetic understanding. "I'm certain he truly cares for you. If you try hard enough, I know you will find a way to work out your problems. You make such a lovely couple."

"I—" Rachel was dumbfounded and lost for words.

But the woman didn't expect her to say anything. "Poppa and I have had our share of arguments over the years. Sometimes he has made me so angry that I didn't want to see him again, but it passes," she assured Rachel. "No marriage is wonderful all the time. In fact, often it is only some of the time." A tiny smile touched her mouth as she confided her experience.

"I'm sure that's true." Rachel's expression softened. There were always highs and lows, but most of the time marriages were on a level plateau.

"One thing I do know," the woman insisted with a scolding shake of her finger. "You will solve nothing by sleeping in one cabin while your husband sleeps in another."

At last Rachel understood what this was all about. The woman had obviously seen the corrected passenger list and noticed that Gard was in a different cabin. She tried very hard not to smile.

"I'm sure everything will work out for the best. Thank you for caring," she murmured.

"Just remember what I said," the woman reminded her and toddled off.

CHAPTER SIX

PUNCTUALITY HAD always been important to Rachel. At half past seven on the dot she walked into the passageway running lengthwise of the Bridge Deck and stopped at the first door on her right. It stood open, the sound of voices coming from inside the suite, signaling the arrival of other guests ahead of her.

Uncertain whether to knock or just walk in, Rachel hesitated, then opted for the latter and walked into the suite unannounced. Four ship's officers in white uniforms were standing with Gard in the large sitting room, drinks in hand while they munched on the assorted cheeses and hors d'oeuvres arranged on trays on a round dining table.

When Gard turned and saw her, a smile touched the corners of his eyes. He separated himself from the group and crossed the room to greet her. Although Rachel was used to being the lone woman in business meetings, the feeling was different in a social situation.

"You did say seven thirty," she said to Gard, conscious of the smiling stares of the, so far, all-male guests.

"I did." He nodded as his gaze swept over her dress, patterned in an updated version of a turn-of-the-century style out of a raspberry-ice crepe.

The high-buttoned collar rose above a deeply veed yoke created by tiny rows of pleated tucks and outlined with a ruffle. The tucks and ruffles were repeated again in the cuffs of the long sleeves. A narrow sash, tied in a bow at her waist, let the soft material flow to a knee-length skirt. In keeping with the dress's style, Rachel had loosely piled her ebony-dark hair onto her head in an upsweep. A muted shade of raspberry eye shadow on her lids brought a hint of amethyst into the soft gray of her eyes.

"You look lovely," Gard said with a quirking smile that matched the dryly amused gleam in his eyes. "But I can't help wondering if that touch-me-not dress you're wearing is supposed to give me a message.''

His remark made Rachel wonder if she hadn't subconsciously chosen this particular dress, which covered practically every inch of her body, for that very reason. But that would indicate that she felt sexually threatened by her own inner desires, which she was trying to keep locked in.

''Hardly,'' she replied. ''You'd probably see it as a challenge.''

''You could be right there,'' he conceded, then took her by the arm to lead her over to his other guests. ''I have some friends I'd like you to meet.''

He introduced her to the four officers, including the purser, Jake Franklin, whom she'd already met. But it was Gard's close friend, Hank Scarborough, who put a quick end to polite formalities and meaningless phrases of acknowledged introductions.

''Ever since I heard about you, Mrs. MacKinley, I've been anxious to meet you.'' Hank Scarborough was Gard's age, in his middle to late thirties, not quite as tall and more compactly built, with sandy-fair hair and an engaging smile. There was a gleam of deviltry in his eye that seemed to hint that he was fond of a good story. "You more than live up to your reputation."

"Thank you," Rachel said, not sure whether she should take that as a compliment.

"I admit I was curious about a woman who would first pass herself off as Gard's wife, then boot him out of his own cabin with not so much as a 'by your leave.'" He grinned to let her see that he knew the whole story and the unusual circumstances. His mocking glance slid to Gard. "You should have kept her for your wife."

"Give me time, Hank," he advised.

A sliver of excitement pierced Rachel's calm at Gard's easy and confident reply. She had to remind herself that he was just going along with the razzing. It did not necessarily mean that he was developing a serious interest in her. When his dark gaze swung to her, she was able to meet it smoothly.

"What would you like to drink?" Gard asked and let his gaze skim her nearly Victorian dress. "Sherry, perhaps?" he mocked.

"I'll have a gin and tonic," she ordered.

There was a subdued cheer from the officers. "A good British drink." They applauded her choice. "You'll fit right in with the rest of us chaps."

By the time Gard had mixed her drink, other guests had begun to arrive for the private cocktail party. It wasn't long before the large sitting room was crowded wall-to-wall with people. The captain stopped in for a few minutes, entertaining Rachel and some of the other guests with his dry British wit.

It seemed the party had barely started when it was interrupted with the announcement that dinner was being served in the Coral Dining Room. There was an unhurried drifting of guests out of the suite. Rachel would have joined the general exodus, but she had been cornered by Hank Scarborough and found herself listening to a long, detailed account of his life at sea.

The last guest had left before Gard came to her rescue. "You've monopolized her long enough, Hank," he said and casually curved an arm around her waist to draw her away. "I'm taking the lady to dinner."

"I suppose you must," Hank declared with a mock sigh of regret. "I'll have the steward come in and clean up this mess. The two of you run along."

Rachel became suspicious of the glance they exchanged. As Gard walked her out to the elevators she eyed him with a speculating look.

"You arranged it with Hank to keep me detained so you could take me down to dinner, didn't you?" she accused with a knowing look.

His mouth was pulled in a mockingly grim line. "I'll have to have a talk with Hank. He wasn't supposed to be so obvious about it," Gard replied, virtually admitting that had been his ploy.

She laughed softly, not really minding that it had all been set up. The elevator doors opened noiselessly and Rachel stepped into the cubicle ahead of Gard.

Dinner was followed by a Parisian show at the Carousel Lounge and, later, dancing. All of which Rachel enjoyed in Gard's company. A midnight buffet snack was being served in the aft portion of the Riviera Deck. Gard tried to tempt her into sampling some of the cakes and sweets, but she resisted.

"No." She avoided the buffet table and kept an unswerving course to the stairs. "It's time to call it a night," she insisted, tired yet feeling a pleasant glow that accompanied a most enjoyable evening.

"Would you like to take a stroll around the deck before turning in?" Gard asked as they climbed the stairs, stopping at the Promenade Deck, where her cabin was located.

"No, not tonight," Rachel refused with visions of last night's embrace on the outer deck dancing in her head.

When they reached the door to her cabin, Rachel turned and leaned a shoulder against it to bid him good night. Gard leaned a forearm against the door by her head, bending slightly toward her and closing the distance between them. She tipped her head back in quiet languor and let it rest against the solid door while she gazed at him. There was a pleasant tingle of sensation as his glance drifted to her lips.

"You could always invite me in and ring the steward for some coffee," he murmured the suggestion.

"I could." Her reply was pitched in an equally soft voice as she began to study the smooth line of his mouth, so strong and warm. Rachel knew the wayward direction her thoughts were taking, but she had no desire to check them from their forbidden path.

"Well?" Gard prompted lazily.

Regardless of what she was thinking, she said, "I could, but I'm not going to ask you to come inside."

His rueful smile seemed to indicate that her decision was not at all unexpected. "Maybe you're right. That single bed would be awfully tight quarters."

A little shiver of excitement raced over her skin at such an open admission of his intention. When his head began a downward movement, blood surged into her heart, swelling it until it seemed to fill her whole chest. Her lips lifted to eliminate the last inch that separated her from his mouth.

The hard, male length of him was against her, pinning her body to the door with his pressing weight. His hand lay familiarly on her hip bone while his kiss probed the dark recesses of her mouth with evocative skill. Beneath her hands she could feel the warmth of his skin through the silk dress shirt. Some sensitive inner radar picked up the increased rate of his breathing.

The tangling intimacy of the deep kiss aroused an insistent hunger that made her ache inside. Rachel strained to satisfy this trembling need by responding more fiercely to his kiss. But a much more intimate union was required before the aching throb of her flesh could know gratification.

She sensed his shared frustration as Gard abandoned his ravishment of her lips and trained his rough kisses on the hollow behind her ear and the ultrasensitive cord in her neck. She gritted her teeth to hold silent the moan that rose in her throat. It came out in a shuddering sigh.

His hand moved up her waist and cupped the underswell of her breast in the span of his thumb and fingers. The thrilling touch seemed to fill her with an explosive desire. The deep breath she took merely caused her breasts to lift and press more fully into his caress.

There was a labored edge to his breathing when his mouth halted near her ear. "Are you sure you don't want to change your mind about that coffee?" Gard asked on a groaning underbreath.

Inside she was trembling badly—wanting just that. But she was afraid she wanted it too badly. It was the desires of the flesh that were threatening to rule her. She'd sooner listen to her heart or her head than something so base.

"No," Rachel answered with a little gulp of air and finally let her closed lashes open. "No coffee." Her hand exerted a slight pressure to end the embrace.

There was an instant when Gard stiffened to keep her pinned to the door. His dark eyes smoldered with sensual promise while he warred with his indecision—whether to believe her words or the unmistakable signals he received from her body. Rachel watched him; slowly he eased himself away, his jawline hardening with grim reluctance.

"You make things hard for a man," he muttered in faint accusation.

"I know," she admitted guiltily. "I—"

He put his fingers to her mouth, silencing her next words. "For God's sake, don't say you're sorry." His finger traced over the softness of her lips, then moved off at a corner and came under her chin, rubbing the point of it with his knuckles.

"All right, I won't," Rachel agreed softly because she wasn't truly sorry about the open way she had responded to him.

"Good night, Rachel." There was a split-second's hesitation before he caught the point of her chin between his thumb and finger, holding it still while his mouth swooped down and brushed across her lips in a fleeting kiss.

"Good night," she managed to reply after he was standing well clear of her.

Under his watchful eye she turned and shakily removed the key from her evening purse to insert it in the lock. Before she entered the cabin, Rachel glanced over her shoulder once and smiled faintly at him, then stepped inside.

For a long moment she leaned against the closed door and held on to the lingering after-sensations, trying to separate emotional from physical pleasure. They were too deeply merged for her introspective study to divide.

Slowly Rachel moved away from the door into the center of the room. All the preparations for her retirement had already been made by the night steward—the bed was turned down and the drapes were closed. The next day's issue of the *Princess Patter* was on the table.

Rachel slipped off her silver-gilt shoes and set them on a chair cushion with the matching evening purse. She reached behind her neck and began to unfasten the tiny eyehooks of the dress's high collar. The first one slipped free easily, but the second was more stubborn.

"Damn," she swore softly in frustration, unable to see what she was doing and obliged to rely on feel alone.

"Need some help?" Gard's lazy voice sounded behind her.

Startled, she swiveled around, her fingers still at the back of her collar. He stood silently inside her cabin door and calmly pushed it shut. Wide-eyed, she watched him, certain the door had been locked and the key replaced in her purse.

"How did you get in here?" She finally managed to overcome her surprise and shock and ask him the question.

"I had a key to this cabin to start out with—remember?" There was a glint in his eye as he crossed the room to where she stood. "For some reason I...haven't remembered to turn it in." He held it up between his thumb and forefinger to show her. "I decided it was time I removed temptations from my pocket."

It hadn't occurred to Rachel that Gard still might have a key to the cabin they had shared so briefly. When he offered it to her, she extended an upturned palm to receive it. The metal key felt warm against her skin when Gard laid it in the center of her palm. Her hand closed around it as her silently questioning gaze searched his face.

"You could just as easily have knocked," Rachel said.

"I could have," he admitted as his glance went to the hand still clutching the back neckline of her dress. No apology was offered for the fact that he had let himself in. "I guess I didn't want to have the door shut on me again.''

Her eyes ran over him, taking in the masculinity of his form and finding pleasure in the presence of a man in her room...in her life.

"I think you'd better leave now." Her suggestion was completely at odds with what she was feeling.

"Not yet." His mouth quirked. "First I'll help you with those hooks. Turn around."

Rachel hesitated, then slowly turned her back to him and tipped her head down. Her stomach churned with nervous excitement at the firm touch of his fingers on the nape of her neck.

"If nothing else," Gard murmured dryly, "I'll have the satisfaction of doing this...even if it means the cold comfort of a shower afterward."

The material around her throat was loosened as he unfastened the three remaining hooks that held the high collar. An aroused tension swept through her system when she felt his fingers on the zipper. He slowly ran it down to the bottom, the sensation of his touch trailing the length of her spine. With a hand crossed diagonally, Rachel held the front of her raspberry dress to her body.

His hands rested lightly on each shoulder bone. She felt the stirring warmth of his breath against the bared skin of her neck an instant before his warm mouth investigated the nape of her neck, finding the pleasure point where all sensation was heightened to a rawly exciting pitch. Her mouth went dry as a weakness attacked her knees. Somehow she managed to hold herself upright without sagging against him.

"I think you'd better leave, Gard." Rachel didn't dare turn around, because she knew if she did, she'd go right into his arms.

Disappointment welled in her throat when he moved away from her and walked to the door. But he paused there, waiting for her to look at him. When she did, Rachel was glad of the distance that made the longing in her eyes less naked.

"I never did get around to giving you a tour of the owner's suite," Gard said. "It has a double bed."

"Does it?" Her voice was shaking a little.

"Next time I'll invite you to my place...for coffee," he added on an intimate note and opened the door.

When it had closed behind him, Rachel discovered she was gripping the extra key in her hand. She looked at it for a long moment, almost wishing he had it back. A degree of sanity returned and she slipped the key into her purse with its mate.

RACHEL STOOD at the bow in front of the wheel-house as the ship steamed into the inlet of the bustling Mazatlán Harbor. High on a hill, the massive lighthouse of El Faro kept a watchful eye on the ship while shrimp boats passed by on their way out to sea.

"Are you going ashore when we dock?" Gard asked, coming up behind her.

She really wasn't surprised to see him. In fact, she'd been expecting him. "Yes, I am." She cast a glance at him, the vividness of last night's interlude still claiming her senses.

In denims and a pale blue shirt, he looked bronzed and rugged. Those hard, smooth features were irresistibly handsome. Rachel wondered if she didn't need her head examined for taking it so slow.

"Did you sign up for one of the tours?"

"No." She shook her head briefly and tucked her hair behind an ear, almost a defensive gesture to ward off the intensity of his gaze. "I thought I'd explore on my own."

"Would you like a private guide?" Gard asked. "I know where you can hire one—cheap."

"Does he speak English?" She guessed he was offering his services, but she went along with his gambit, albeit tongue-in-cheek.

"*Sí, señorita,*" he replied in an exaggerated Mexican dialect. "And *español,* too."

"How expensive?" Rachel challenged.

"Let's just say—no more than you're willing to pay," Gard suggested.

"That sounds fair." She nodded and felt the run of breathless excitement through her system.

"We'll go ashore after breakfast," he said. "Be sure to wear your swimsuit under your clothes. We'll do our touring in the morning and spend the afternoon on the beach."

"Sounds wonderful."

WHEN THEY went ashore, Gard rented a three-wheeled cart, open on all sides, to take them to town. As he explained to Rachel, it was called a *pulmonía*, which meant "pneumonia" because of its openness to the air.

Their tour through town took them past the town square with its statue of a deer. Mazatlán was an Indian name meaning "place of the deer." Gard directed their driver to take them past the Temple of San Jose, the church constructed by the Spanish during their reign in Mexico. Afterward he had the driver let them off at El Mercado.

They spent the balance of the morning wandering through the maze of stalls and buildings. The range of items for sale was endless. There were butcher shops with sides of beef and scrawny plucked chickens dangling from hooks, and fruit stands and vegetable stands. And there was an endless array of crafts shops, souvenir stores, and clothing items.

For lunch Gard took her to one of the restaurants along the beach. When Rachel discovered their seafood had been caught fresh that morning, she feasted on shrimp, the most succulent and flavorful she'd ever tasted.

Later, sitting on a beach towel with an arm hooked around a raised knee, Rachel watched the gentle surf breaking on shore. After the morning tour and the delicious lunch, she didn't have the energy to do more than laze on the beach. Gard was stretched out on another beach towel beside her, a hand over his eyes to block out the sun. It had been a long time since he'd said anything. Rachel wondered if he was sleeping.

Off to her left an old, bowlegged Mexican vendor shuffled into view. Dressed in the typical loose shirt and baggy trousers with leather huaraches, he ambled toward Rachel and held up a glass jar half-filled with water. Fire opals gleamed on the bottom.

"Señora?" He offered them to her for inspection.

"No, thank you." She shook her head to reinforce her denial.

"Very cheap," he insisted, but she shook her head again. He leaned closer and reached into his back pocket. "I have a paper—you buy."

Gard said something in Spanish. The old man shrugged and put the folded paper back in his pocket, then shuffled on down the beach. Rachel cast a curious glance at Gard.

"What was he selling?" she asked.

"A treasure map." He propped himself up on an elbow. "This harbor was a favorite haunt of pirates. Supposedly there're caches of buried treasure all over this area. You'd be surprised how many 'carefully aged' maps have been supposedly found just last week in some old chest in the attic." There was a dryly cynical gleam of amusement in his eyes.

"And they're for sale—cheap—to anyone foolish enough to buy them." Rachel understood the rest of the game.

Turning the upper half of her body, she reached into the beach bag sitting on the grainy sand behind her and took out the bottle of sun oil lying atop their folded clothes. She uncapped the bottle and began to smooth the oil on her legs and arms.

There was a shift of movement beside her as Gard again stretched out flat and crooked an arm under his head for a pillow. His eyes were closed against the glare of the high afternoon sun. With absent movements Rachel continued to spread the oil over her exposed flesh while her gaze wandered over the bronze sheen of his longly muscled body, clad in white-trimmed navy swimming trunks.

The urge, ever since he'd stripped down, had been to touch him and have that sensation of hard, vital flesh beneath her hands. It was unnerving and stimulating to look at him.

"Enjoying yourself?" His low taunt startled Rachel.

Her gaze darted from his leanly muscled thighs to his face, but his eyes were still closed, so he couldn't know she had been staring at him. His question was obviously referring to something else.

"Of course." She attempted to inject a brightness in her voice. "It's a gorgeous day and the beach is quiet and uncrowded."

"That isn't what I meant, and you know it." The amused mockery in his voice had a faint sting to it. "I could feel the way you were staring at me, and I wondered if you liked what you saw."

Rachel was a little uncomfortable at being caught admiring his male body. She concentrated all her attention on rubbing the oil over an arm.

"Yes." She kept her answer simple, but some other comment was required. "I suppose you're used to women staring at you." It was a light remark, meant to tease him for seeking a compliment from her.

"Why? Because I could feel your eyes on me?" Gard shifted his dark head on the pillow of his arm to look at her. "Can't you feel it when I look at you?"

The rush of heat over her skin had nothing to do with the hot sun overhead. It was a purely sexual sensation caused by the boldness of his gaze. It was a look that did not just strip her bathing suit away. His eyes were making love to her, touching and caressing every hidden point and hollow of her body. It left her feeling too shaken and vulnerable.

"Don't." The low word vibrated from her and asked him to stop, protesting the way it was destroying her.

The contact was abruptly broken. "Hand me my cigarettes," Gard said with a degree of terseness. "They're in my shirt pocket."

Rachel wiped the excess oil from her hand on a towel and tried to stop her hand from shaking as she reached inside the beach bag,

then handed him the pack of cigarettes and a
lighter. She leaned back on her hands and
stared at the wave rolling into shore. The silence stretched, broken only by the rustle of
the cigarette pack and the click of the lighter.

"Tell me about your husband," Gard said.

"Mac?" Rachel swung a startled glance at
him, noting the grim set of his mouth and his
absorption with the smoke curling from his
cigarette.

"Is that what you called him?" His hooded
gaze flicked in her direction.

"Yes," she nodded.

"There's consolation in that, I suppose."
His mouth crooked in a dry, humorless line.
"At least I'll have the satisfaction of knowing that when you say my name, you aren't
thinking of someone else."

Rachel's gray eyes grew thoughtful as she
tried to discern whether it was jealousy she
heard or injured pride that came from being
mistaken for someone else.

"What was he like?" Gard repeated his
initial question, then arched her another
glance. "Or would you prefer not to talk
about him?"

"I don't mind," she replied, although she wasn't sure where to begin.

When she looked out to sea, Rachel was looking beyond the farthest point. The edges blurred when she tried to conjure up Mac's image in her mind. It wasn't something recent. It had been happening gradually over the last couple of years. Her memory of him always pictured him as being more handsome than photographs showed. But it was natural for the mind to overlook the flaws in favor of the better qualities.

"Mac was a dynamic, aggressive man," Rachel finally began to describe him, even though she knew her picture of him was no longer accurate. "Even when he was sitting still—which was seldom—he seemed to be all coiled energy. I guess he grabbed at life," she mused, "because he knew he wouldn't be around long." Sighing, she threw a glance at Gard. "It's difficult to describe Mac to someone who didn't know him."

"You loved him?"

"Everyone loved Mac," she declared with a faint smile. "He was hearty and warm. Yes, I loved him."

"Are you still married to him?" Gard asked flatly. Rachel frowned at him blankly, finding his question strange. A sardonic light flashed in his dark eyes before he swung his gaze away from her to inhale on his cigarette. "Even after their husbands die, some women stay married to their ghosts."

The profundity of his remark made Rachel stop and think. Although she had wondered many times if she would ever feel so strongly for another man again, she hadn't locked out the possibility. She wrapped her arms around her legs and hugged them to her chest, resting her chin on her knees.

"No," she said after a moment. "I'm not married to Mac's ghost." Her glance ran sideways to him. "Why did you ask?"

"I wondered if that was the reason you didn't want me in your cabin last night." Gard released a short breath, rife with impatient disgust. "I wonder if you realize how hard it was for me to leave last night."

"You shouldn't have come in." Rachel refused to let him put the onus of his difficulty on her.

"I'm not pointing any fingers." Gard sat up, bringing his gaze eye-level with hers. She was uncomfortable with his hard and probing look. "I'm just trying to figure you out."

There was something in the way he said it that ruffled her fur. "Don't strain yourself," she flashed tightly.

Amusement flickered lazily in his eyes. "You've been a strain on me from the beginning."

In her opinion the conversation was going nowhere. "I think I'll go in the water for a swim," Rachel announced and rolled to her feet.

"That's always your solution, isn't it?" Gard taunted, and Rachel paused to look back at him, wary and vaguely upset. "When a situation gets too hot and uncomfortable for you, you walk away. You know I want to make love to you." He said it as casually as if he were talking about the weather.

There was a haughty arch of one eyebrow as her eyes turned iron-gray and cool. "You aren't the first." She saw the flare of anger, but she turned and walked to the sea, wading in, then diving into the curl of an oncoming wave. There was a definite sense of anger at the idea that simply because he had expressed a desire for her, she was supposed to fall into his arms. If anything, his remark had driven her away from him.

Rachel swam with energy, going against the surf the same way she went against her own natural inclination. Eventually she tired and let the tide float her back to shore where Gard waited. But the tense scene that had passed before had created a strain between them that wasn't easily relieved.

CHAPTER SEVEN

ALONE, RACHEL strolled along a street in downtown Puerto Vallarta, the second port of call of the *Pacific Princess*. As it had yesterday, the ship had berthed early in the morning. This time Rachel settled for the continental breakfast served on the Sun Deck and disembarked as soon as the formalities with the Mexican port authorities were observed and permission was given to let passengers go ashore.

To herself she claimed it was a desire to explore the picturesque city on her own. It was merely a side benefit that she hadn't seen Gard before she'd left the ship. Common sense told her the coolness that had come between them yesterday was a good thing. She needed time to step back and look at the relationship to see whether she'd been swept along by a strong emotional current or if she'd been caught in a maelstrom of physical desire.

Few of the shops were open before nine, so Rachel idled away the time looking in windows and eyeing the architecture of the buildings. At intersections she had views of the surrounding hills where the city had sprawled high onto their sides, creating streets that were San Francisco steep.

Something shimmered golden and bright against the skyline. When Rachel looked to see what it was, a breath was indrawn in awed appreciation. The morning sunlight was reflecting off the gold crown of a steeple and making it glow as if with its own golden light.

With this landmark in sight Rachel steered a course toward it for a closer look. Two blocks farther she reached the source. It was the cathedral of Our Lady of Guadalupe. The doors of the church stood invitingly open at the top of concrete steps, but it continued to be the crown that drew Rachel's gaze as she stood near the church's base with her head tipped back to stare admiringly at it.

"It's a replica of the crown worn by the Virgin in the Basilica at Mexico City."

At the sound of Gard's voice, Rachel jerked her gaze downward and found him, leaning casually against a concrete side of the church steps and smoking a cigarette. She felt the sudden rush of her pulse under the lazy and knowing inspection of his dark eyes. The cigarette was dropped beneath his heel and crushed out as he pushed away and came toward her. A quiver of awareness ran through her senses at his malely lean physique clad in butternut-brown slacks and a cream-yellow shirt.

"I've been waiting for you to turn up," Gard said calmly.

The certainty in his tone implied that he had known she would. It broke her silence. "How could you possibly know I would come here?" Rachel demanded with a rush of anger. "I didn't even know it."

"It was a calculated risk," he replied, looking at her eyes and appearing to be amused by the silver sparks shooting through their grayness. "Puerto Vallarta basically doesn't have much in the way of historical or cultural attractions. It's too early for most of the shops to be open, so you had to be wandering around, looking at the sights. Which meant, sooner or later, you'd find your way here.''

It didn't help her irritation to find that his assumption was based on well thought out logic. ''Always presuming I had come ashore.'' There was a challenging lift to her voice.

''Don't forget''—a slow, easy smile deepened the grooves running parenthetically at the corners of his mouth—''I know most of the officers and crew from the bridge, including the man on duty at the gangway. He told me you were one of the first to go ashore this morning. I have spies everywhere.''

His remark was offered in jest, but Rachel wasn't amused. ''So it would seem,'' she said curtly, reacting to the threading tension that was turning her nerves raw. His sudden appearance had thrown her off balance.

''Would you like to see the inside of the cathedral?'' Gard inquired, smoothly ignoring her shortness and acting as if there hadn't been any cool constraint between them.

''No.'' She swung away from the church steps and began to walk along the narrow sidewalk in the direction of the shopping district.

"I rented a car for the day." He fell in step with her, letting her gaze slide over her profile.

"Good for you." Rachel continued to look straight ahead. She felt slightly short of breath and knew it wasn't caused by the leisurely pace of her steps.

"I thought we could drive around and see the sights." There was a heavy run of amusement in his voice.

She tossed a glance in his direction that didn't quite meet his sidelong study of her. Some of her poise was returning, taking the abrasive edge out of her voice. But it didn't lessen her resentment at the way Gard was taking it for granted that she would want to spend the day with him—just as yesterday when he had taken it for granted that because he had expressed a desire to make love to her, she should have been wildly impressed.

"I thought you just said there weren't any sights to see in Puerto Vallarta," she reminded him coolly.

"I said there weren't any major cultural attractions," Gard corrected her. "But there's plenty of scenery. I thought we could drive around town, maybe stop to see some friends of mine—they have a place in Gringo Gulch where a lot of Americans have vacation homes—then drive out in the country."

"It's a shame you went to so much trouble planning out the day's activities for *us* without consulting me," Rachel informed him with honeyed sweetness. "I could have told you that I'd already made plans and you wouldn't have wasted your time."

"Oh?" His glance was mildly interested, a touch of skepticism in his look. "What kind of plans have you made?"

Rachel had to think quickly, because her plans were haphazard at best. "I planned to do some shopping this morning. There're several good sportswear lines that are made here, and I want to pick up some small gifts for friends back home."

"And the afternoon?" Gard prompted.

The beach bag she carried made that answer rather obvious. "I'm going to the beach."

"Any particular beach?"

"No." Her gaze remained fixed to the front, but she wasn't seeing much. All her senses were tuned to the man strolling casually at her side.

"I know a quiet, out-of-the-way spot. We'll go there this afternoon after you've finished your shopping."

"Look." Rachel stopped abruptly in the middle of the sidewalk to confront him. Gard was slower to halt, then came halfway around to partially face her. His handsomely hewn features showed a mild, questioning surprise at this sudden stop. "I'm not going with you this afternoon."

"Why?" He seemed untroubled by her announcement.

There was frustration in knowing that she didn't have an adequate reason. Even more damnably frustrating was the knowledge that she wouldn't mind being persuaded to alter her plans. She became all the more determined to resist such temptation.

"Because I've made other plans." Rachel chose a terse non-answer and began to walk again.

"Then I'll go along with you." With a diffident shrug of his shoulders, Gard fell in with her plans.

She flicked him an impatient glance. "Are you in the habit of inviting yourself when you're not asked?"

"On occasion," he admitted with a hint of a complacent smile.

More shops were beginning to unlock their doors to open for business. Out of sheer perversity Rachel attempted to bore him by wandering in and out of every store, not caring whether it was a silversmith or a boutique, whether it sold copper and brassware or colorful Mexican pottery.

Yet she never detected any trace of impatience as he lounged inside a store's entrance while she browsed through its merchandise. She did make a few small purchases: a hand-embroidered blouse for Mrs. Pollock next door, and two ceramic figurines of Joseph and Mary riding a donkey for Fan's collection of Christmas decorations. Gard offered to carry them for her, but she stubbornly tucked them inside her beach bag.

In the next boutique she entered, Rachel found a two-piece beach cover-up patterned in exactly the same shade of lavender as her swimsuit. The sales clerk showed her the many ways the wraparound skirt could be worn, either long with its midriff-short blouse or tied sarong fashion. After haggling good-naturedly over the price for better than half an hour, Rachel bought the outfit.

"You drive a hard bargain," Gard observed dryly as he followed her out of the store.

Bargaining over the price was an accepted practice in most of Mexico, especially when a particular item wasn't marked with a price, so Rachel was a little puzzled why he was commenting on her negotiation for a lower price.

"It's business," she countered.

"I agree," he conceded. "But you practiced it like you were an old hand at negotiating for a better price."

"I suppose I am." She smiled absently, because she was often involved in negotiating better prices for bulk-order purchases of furniture or related goods for her company. "It's part of my work."

"I didn't realize you worked." Gard looked at her with frowning interest.

Rachel laughed shortly. "You surely didn't think my only occupation was that of a widow?"

"I suppose I did." He shrugged and continued to study her. "I didn't really give it much thought. What do you do?"

"I own a small chain of retail furniture stores." Her chin lifted slightly in a faint show of pride.

"If they're managed properly, they can be a sound investment." The comment was idly made. "Who have you hired to handle the management of them for you?"

"No one." Rachel challenged him with her glance. "I manage them myself."

"I see." His expression became closed, withdrawing any reaction to her announcement. That, in itself, was an indication of his skepticism toward her ability to do the job well.

"I suppose you think a woman can't run a business," she murmured, fuming silently.

"I didn't say that."

"You didn't have to!" she flared.

"You took me by surprise, Rachel." Gard attempted to placate her flash of temper with calm reasoning. "Over the years I've met a few successful female executives. You just don't look the type."

"And what is the type?" Hot ice crystallized in her voice as she threw him a scathing look. "Ambitious and cold and wearing jackets with padded shoulders?" She didn't wait for him to answer as her lips came thinly together in disgust. "That is the most sexist idea I've ever heard!"

"That isn't what I meant at all, but the point is well taken," he conceded with a bemused light at his dusty brown eyes. "I deserved that for generalizing."

She was too angry to care that Gard admitted he'd been wrong. She turned on him. "Why don't you go back to the ship...or go drive around in your rented car? Go do whatever it is that you want to do and leave me alone! I'm tired of you following me!"

"I was wrong and I apologize," Gard repeated with a smooth and deliberately engaging smile. "Let's find a restaurant and have some lunch."

"You simply don't listen, do you?" she declared in taut anger and looked rawly around the immediate vicinity.

A uniformed police officer was standing on the corner only a few yards away. Rachel acted on impulse, without pausing to think through the idea. In a running walk she swept past Gard and hurried toward the policeman.

"Officer?" she called to attract his attention.

He turned, his alert, dark eyes immediately going to her. He was of medium height with a stocky, muscular build. His broad features had a no-nonsense look, reinforced by a full black mustache. He walked to meet Rachel as she approached him, his gaze darting behind her to Gard.

"Officer, this man is annoying me." Rachel turned her accusing glance on Gard as he leisurely came up to stand behind her.

His expression continued to exhibit patience, but there was a hard glint in his eyes, too, at her new tactic. When she looked back at the policeman, Rachel wasn't sure he had understood her.

"This man has been following me." She gestured toward Gard. "I want him to stop it and leave me alone."

"The *señor* makes trouble for you?" the officer repeated in a thick accent to be certain he had understood.

"Yes," Rachel nodded, then added for further clarification, "*Sí.*"

The policeman turned a cold and narrowed look on Gard while Rachel watched with cool satisfaction. He started to address Gard, but Gard broke in, speaking in an unhesitating Spanish. The policeman's expression underwent a rapid change, going from a stern to a faintly amused look.

"What did you say to him?" Rachel demanded from Gard.

"I merely explained that we've had a small argument." The hard challenge continued to show behind his smiling look. "I was tired of shopping and wanted some lunch. And you— my wife—insisted on going through more stores first."

Her mouth opened on a breath of anger, but she didn't waste it on Gard. Instead she swung to the officer. "That isn't true," she denied. "I am not his wife. I've never seen him before in my life."

An obviously puzzled officer looked once more to Gard. *"Señor?"*

There was another explanation in Spanish that Rachel couldn't understand, but it was followed by Gard reaching into his pocket, and producing identification. The edge was taken off her anger with the dawning realization of how she was being trapped.

"Would you care to show him your passport or driver's license, Mrs. MacKinley?" Gard taunted softly.

"Señora, your papers?" the officer requested.

Dully she removed her passport from the zippered compartment in her purse and showed it to him. A grimly resigned look showed her acceptance of defeat for the way Gard had outmaneuvered her. With the difficulties of the language barrier, she couldn't hope to convincingly explain that even though their surnames were the same, they weren't related.

When the policeman returned the passport, he observed her subdued expression. It was plain that he considered this a domestic matter, not requiring his intervention. He made some comment to Gard and grinned before touching a hand to his hat in a salute and moving to the side.

"What did he say?" Rachel demanded.

Before she could tighten her hold on the beach bag, filled to the top now with her morning's purchases, Gard was taking it from her and gripping her arm just above the elbow to propel her down the sidewalk. Rachel resisted, but with no success.

"He was recommending a restaurant where we could have lunch," he replied tautly, ignoring her attempts to pull free of his grasp.

"I'm not hungry," she muttered.

"I seem to have lost my appetite, too." His fingers tightened, digging into her flesh as he steered her around a corner.

The line of his jaw was rigid, hard flesh stretched tautly across it. Her own mouth was clamped firmly shut, refusing to make angry feminine pleas to be released. She stopped actively struggling against his grip and instead held herself stiff, not yielding to his physical force.

Halfway down the narrow cross street he pulled her to a stop beside a parked car and opened the door. "Get in," he ordered.

Rachel flashed him another angry glance, but he didn't let go of her arm until she was sitting in the passenger seat. Then he closed the door and walked around to the driver's side. She toyed with the idea of jumping out of the car, but it sounded childish even to her. Her beach bag was tossed into the back seat as Gard slid behind the wheel and inserted the key into the ignition switch.

Holding her tight-lipped silence, she said nothing as he turned into the busy traffic on the Malecon, the main thoroughfare in Puerto Vallarta, which curved along the waterfront of Banderas Bay. At the bridge over the Cuale River the traffic became heavier as cabs, trucks, burros, and bicycles all vied to cross.

The river was also the local laundromat. Rachel had a glimpse of natives washing their clothes and their children in the river below when Gard took his turn crossing the bridge. Under other circumstances she would have been fascinated by this bit of local atmosphere, but as it was, she saw it and forgot it.

Her sense of direction had always been excellent. Without being told, she knew they were going in the exactly opposite direction of the pier where the ship was tied. It was on the north side of town and they were traveling south. The road began to climb and twist up the mountainside that butted the sea, past houses and sparkling white condominiums clinging to precarious perches on the steep bluffs. When the resorts and residences began to thin out, Gard still didn't slow down.

Rachel couldn't stand the oppressive silence any longer. "Am I being abducted?"

"You might call it that," was Gard's clipped answer.

Not once since he'd climbed behind the wheel had his gaze strayed from the road. His profile seemed to be chiseled out of teak, carved in unrelenting lines. She looked at the sure grip of his hands on the steering wheel. Her arm felt bruised from the steely force of his fingers, but she refused to mention the lingering soreness.

As they rounded the mountain the road began a downward curve to a sheltered bay with a large sandy beach and a scattering of build-

ings and resorts. Recalling his earlier invitation to spend the afternoon in some quiet
beach area, Rachel wondered if this was it.

"Is that where we're going?" The tension
stayed in her voice, giving it an edge.

"No." His gaze flashed over the bay and
returned to the road, the uncompromising set
of his features never changing. "That's where
they filmed the movie *The Night of the
Iguana.*" His voice was flat and hard.

"You can let me off there," Rachel stated
and stared straight ahead. "I should be able
to hire a taxi to take me back to town."

There was a sudden braking of the car. Rachel braced a hand against the dashboard to
keep from being catapulted forward as Gard
swerved the car off the road and onto a layby
next to some building ruins overlooking the
bay.

While Rachel was still trying to figure out
what was happening, the motor was switched
off and the emergency brake was pulled on.
When Gard swung around to face her, an arm
stretching along the seatback behind her
head, she grabbed for the door handle.

"Oh, no, you don't," he growled as his snaring hand caught her wrist before she could pull the door handle.

"Damn you, let me go!" Rachel tried to pry loose from his grip with her free hand, but he caught it, too, and jerked her toward him.

"I'm not letting you go until we get a few things straight," Gard stated through his teeth.

"Go to hell." She was blazing mad.

So was Gard. That lazy, easygoing manner she was so accustomed to seeing imprinted on his features was nowhere to be seen. He was all hard and angry, his dark eyes glittering with a kind of violence. He had stopped turning the other cheek. Recognizing this, Rachel turned wary—no longer hitting out at him now that she discovered he was capable of retaliating. But it was too late.

"If I'm going to hell, you're coming with me," he muttered thickly.

He yanked her closer, a muscled arm going around her and trapping her arms between them as he crushed her to his chest. His fingers roughly twisted into her hair, tugging at

the tender roots until her head was forced
back.

When the bruising force of his mouth descended on her lips, Rachel pressed them
tightly shut and strained against the impris-
oning hand that wouldn't permit her to turn
away. The punishment of his kiss seemed to
go on forever. She stopped resisting him so
she could struggle to breathe under his
smothering onslaught. Her heart was pound-
ing in her chest with the effort.

As her body began to go limp with exhaus-
tion the pressure of his mouth changed. A
hunger became mixed with his anger and
ruthlessly devoured her lips. She was sense-
less and weak when he finally dragged his
mouth from hers. Her skin felt fevered from
the soul-destroying fire of the angry kisses.
The heaviness of his breathing swept over her
upturned face as she forced her eyes to open
and look at him.

The fires continued to smolder in his eyes,
now tempered with desirous heat. He studied
her swollen lips with a grimness thinning his
own mouth. The fingers in her hair loosened

their tangling grip that had forced her head backward.

"Woman, you drive me to distraction." The rawly muttered words expressed the same angry desire she saw in his solid features. "Sometimes I wonder if you have any idea just how damned distracting you are!"

Her hands were folded against his muscled chest, burned by the heat of his skin through the thin cotton shirt. She could feel the hard thudding of his heart, so dangerously in tune with the disturbed rhythm of her own pulse. She watched his face, feeling the run of emotions within herself.

"I know that I made you angry yesterday," Gard admitted while his gaze slid to the sun-browned hand on her shoulder. "When I watched you rubbing that lotion over your body, I wanted to do it for you."

As if in recollection, his hand began to glide smoothly over the bareness of her arm. His gaze became fixed on the action while images whirled behind his smoldering dark eyes. Rachel didn't have to see them. She knew what he was imagining because she could visualize the scene, too, and the sensation of his hands moving over her whole body, not just her arm. A churning started in the pit of her stomach and swirled outward.

"But I knew if I touched you"—his gaze flicked to her eyes and looked deeply inside their black orifices—"I wouldn't be able to stop. Instead I had to lie there and pretend it didn't faze me to watch you spread oil all over your skin."

She dropped her gaze, unwilling to comment. It was disturbing to look back on the scene yesterday on the beach and know what he was thinking and feeling at the time.

"And I've made you angry this morning," Gard continued on a firmer note. "I never claimed to be without flaws, but dammit, I want to spend the day with you. Do you want to spend the day with me? And answer me honestly."

When she met his gaze, she had the feeling she was a hostile witness being cross-examined by a ruthless attorney and sworn to an oath of truth. Discounting all her petty resentments, Rachel knew what her answer was.

"Yes." She reluctantly forced it out. "Do you always ask such leading questions?"

Some of the hardness went out of his features with the easing of an inner tension. There was even the glint of a smile around his eyes.

"A good lawyer will always lead the conversation in the direction he wants it to go, whether in contract negotiations or court testimony," he admitted. "Unfortunately you objected to the way I was leading."

"But my objection was eventually overruled," Rachel murmured, relenting now that the outcome was known and she had a clearer understanding of why it had happened.

"And you aren't going to appeal the decision?" His mouth quirked.

"Would you listen?" Her voice was falling to a whisper. She wasn't even sure if she knew what they were talking about as his mouth came closer and closer.

It brushed over her tender lips, gently at first, then with increasing warmth until he was sensually absorbing them. His tongue traced their swollen outline and licked away the soreness. Rachel twisted in the seat and arched closer to him, sliding her hands around his neck and spreading her fingers into his hair.

The quarters of the car were too restricting, forcing positions that were too awkward. Breathing heavily, Gard pulled away from her to sit back in the seat. He sent her a dryly amused look.

"It's impossible but every time I get into this with you, the surroundings go from bad to worse," he declared. "Last time it was the dubious comfort of a single bed. Now it's a car seat."

Her laughter was soft; the fire he had ignited was still glowing warm inside her. As he started the car's motor she settled into her own seat.

"You never did tell me where we're going," she reminded him after he had pulled onto the road again.

"Believe it or not"—he turned his head to slide her a look—"I'm taking you to paradise."

"Promises, promises," Rachel teased with a mock sigh.

"You'll see," Gard murmured complacently.

When she looked out the window, she was
amazed to notice how clear and bright the sky
was. The steep mountains were verdantly
green and lush. Below, the ocean rolled
against them in blue waves capped with white
foam. Afterward her gaze was drawn back to
a silent study of Gard. There were flaws, but
none that really mattered.

CHAPTER EIGHT

THEY FOLLOWED the paved road for several more twisting miles before Gard turned onto a short dirt road that led to a parking lot. Rachel read the sign, proclaiming the place as Chico's Paradise.

"I told you I was taking you to paradise," he reminded her as he braked the car to a stop alongside another.

"What is it?" Rachel climbed out of the parked car. The ground seemed to fall away in front of it, but she could see the roof of a building below... several buildings loosely connected, as it turned out. "A restaurant?"

"Among other things," Gard said, being deliberately close-mouthed when he joined her.

Absently Rachel noticed that he was carrying her beach bag, but since they were high in the mountains and some distance from the ocean, she presumed he had brought it rather than leave it in the car where it might possibly be stolen. The lush foliage grew densely around the entrance path, leading down to the buildings. It was barely wide enough for two people to walk abreast.

Gard took her hand and led the way. The first adobe building they passed housed a gift and souvenir shop. Then the path widened into a small courtyard with a fountain and a statue of a naked boy. To the right a woman was making flour tortillas in an open shed area.

It appeared to Rachel that the path dead-ended into an open-air restaurant, but Gard led her through it to a series of stone steps that went down. There was a tangling riot of red bushes that looked to be some relation to the poinciana.

A second later she caught the sound of tumbling, rushing water. She looked in the direction of it. Through the flame-red leaves she saw the cascading waterfall tumbling over stone beds and creating varying levels of rock pools. When she turned her widened eyes to Gard, he was smiling.

"I told you I was taking you to paradise," he murmured softly and offered her the beach bag. "The changing rooms are down here if you want to slip into your swimsuit."

A second invitation wasn't required as she took the beach bag from him and skimmed the top of the steps as she hurried to the small adobe building. When she returned, wearing her lavender swimsuit, Gard had already stripped down to his swimming trunks. He used her beach bag to store his clothes.

Rushing water had worn the huge gray boulders smooth and gouged out holes to make placid pools while the musical cascade of water continued on its way down to the sea. A dozen people were already enjoying the idyllic setting, most of them sunbathing on the warm stone.

"Watch your step," Gard warned when the crudely fashioned steps ended and they had to traverse the massive boulders.

Luckily Rachel had put on her deck shoes. The ridged soles gave her traction to travel over the uneven contours of the huge stones, part of the mountain's core that had been exposed by centuries of carving water. Once they were at the rushing stream's level, Gard turned upstream.

There was no formal path, no easy way to walk along the water's course. Moving singly, they edged around a two-story boulder, flattened against its sheer face with a narrow lip offering toeholds. They passed the main waterfall, where the stream spilled twenty feet into a large, deep pool, and continued upstream. It seemed to require the agility of a mountain goat, climbing and jumping from one stone to another. Sometimes they were forced to leave the stream to circle a standing rock.

No one else had ventured as far as they did, settling for the easy access of the rock pool at the base of the waterfall and the lower-level pools that weren't so difficult to reach. Rachel paused to catch her breath and looked back to see how far they'd come.

The open-air restaurant with its roof of thatched palm leaves sat on the bluff overlooking the main waterfall. Tropical plants crowded around it. At this distance the brilliant scarlet color predominated, looking like clusters of thousands of red flowers.

Almost an equal distance ahead of Rachel she could see a narrow rope bridge crossing the stream. On the other side of the stream there was a knoll where a long adobe house sat in the shade of spreading trees. A large tan dog slept on a patch of cool earth, and from somewhere close by a donkey brayed. But always in the background was the quiet tumble of water on its downward rush to the sea.

"Tired?" Gard's low voice touched her.

"No." Rachel turned, an inner glow lighting her eyes as she met his gaze. "Fascinated."

He passed her a look of understanding and swung back around to lead the way again. "I found a place." The words came over his shoulder as Rachel fell in behind him.

Between two boulders there was a narrow opening and the glistening surface of a mirror-smooth pool just beyond it. Gard squeezed through the opening and disappeared behind one of the boulders. Rachel ventured forward cautiously. From what little she could see of the rock pool, it was walled in by high, sheer stones.

But there was a narrow ledge to the right of the opening that skirted the pool for about four feet. At that point it curved onto another boulder lying on its side, forming a natural deck for the swimming hole. It was secluded and private, guarded by the high rocks surrounding it. Gard stood on the long, relatively flat stones and waited for her to join him.

"Well? Was it worth the walk?" There was a knowing glitter in his eyes when she traversed the last few feet to stand beside him.

"I don't know if I'd call it a 'walk.'" Rachel said, questioning his description of their short trek. "But it was worth it."

His finger hooked under her chin and tipped her head up so he could drop a light kiss on her lips. His lidded gaze continued to study them with disturbing interest, causing a little leap of excitement within Rachel.

"Get your shoes off and let's go for a swim." His low suggestion was at odds with the body signals he was giving, but it seemed wiser to listen to his voice.

"Okay," she breathed out.

While he kicked off his canvas loafers, Rachel sat down on the sun-warmed stone to untie her shoelaces. When both shoes were removed, his hand was there to pull Rachel to her feet. Gard held onto the boulder as he led her down its gentle slope to the pool's edge.

"Is it deep?" She didn't want to dive in without knowing and tentatively stuck a toe in the water to test the temperature. She jerked it back. "The water's cold."

"No," Gard corrected. "The sun is hot, and the water is only warm." His hand tightened its grip on hers and urged her forward. "Come on. Let's jump in."

"Hmm." The negative sound came from her throat as she resisted the pressure of his hand. "You jump in," she said and started to sit down to ease herself slowly into the cool water. "I prefer the gradual shock."

"Oh, no." With a pull of his hand he forced her upright, then scooped her wiggling and protesting body into his arms.

The instant Rachel realized that there was no hope of struggling free, she wrapped her arms around his neck and hung on. "Gard, don't." Her words were halfway between a plea and an empty threat.

There was a complacent gleam in his dark eyes as he looked down at her, cradled in his arms. An awareness curled through her for the sensation of her body curved against the solidness of his naked chest and the hard strength of his flexed arm muscles imprinted on her back and the underside of her legs. It tightened her stomach muscles and closed a hand on her lungs.

Gard sensed the change in her reaction to the moment. A look of intimacy stole into his eyes, too, as his gaze roamed possessively over her face. His body heat seemed to radiate over her skin, warming her flesh the way his look was igniting her desire.

"I'm not going to let you back away this time." His low voice vibrated huskily over her, the comment an obvious reference to the way she had backed away from making love to him. "Sooner or later you're going to have to take the plunge."

"I know," Rachel whispered, because she felt the inevitability of it. At some time or another it had stopped being a question of whether it was what she wanted and become instead when she wanted it to happen.

A smile edged the corners of his mouth. "Damn you for knowing"—his look was alive, gleaming with a mixture of desire and wickedness—"and still putting me through this."

Rachel started to smile, but it froze into place as he suddenly heaved her away from his body. Her hands lost their hold on his neck. For a second there was the sensation of being suspended in air, followed by the shock of cool water encapsulating her body.

Something else hit the water close by her as Rachel kicked for the surface where light glittered. She emerged with a sputtering gasp of air and pushed the black screen of wet hair away from her face and eyes. There was no sign of Gard on the stone bank.

Treading water, Rachel pivoted in a circle to locate him, realizing that he must have dived into the pool after he'd thrown her in. He was behind her, only a couple of yards away. Laughter glinted in his expression.

"It wasn't so traumatic, was it?" mocked Gard.

"A little warning would have been nice," she retorted. "Maybe then I wouldn't have swallowed half the pool."

Now that she'd gotten over the shock, the water seemed pleasantly warm and refreshing. Striking out together, they explored the boundaries of their quiet pool, discovering a small cave hollowed into five feet of solid stone. Its floor was underwater, and the ceiling was too low to allow them to stand inside it.

They stayed in the rock pool for more than an hour, swimming, sometimes floating and talking, sometimes diving to explore the clear depths. Gard climbed out first and helped Rachel onto the stone slab, made slick by the water dripping from their bodies.

Although there were towels in her beach bag, neither made use of them. Instead they sprawled contentedly on the sun-warmed rock and let the afternoon air dry them naturally. Her body felt loose and relaxed as she sat and combed her fingers through the wet tangle of her black hair. She felt tired and exhilarated all at the same time. When she leaned back and braced herself with her hands, she gave a little toss of her head to shake away the wet strands clinging to her neck. It scattered a shower of water droplets onto Gard.

"Hey!" he protested mildly. "You're getting me all wet."

"Look who's complaining about a little water," Rachel mocked him playfully. "You're the same man who threw me into that pool an hour ago."

"That's different." He smiled lazily and raised up on an elbow alongside her.

"That's what I thought." She shifted into a reclining position supported by her elbows. "You can dish it out, but you can't take it."

"It depends on what's being served," Gard corrected and sent an intimating look over her curving figure, outlined by her wet and clinging bathing suit. She felt a response flaring within at his caressing look, but it was wiped from his expression when his gaze returned to her face, a dark brow lifting. "Which reminds me—we never did get around to having lunch."

"That's true. I'd forgotten." Food had been the farthest thing from her mind.

"Are you hungry?"

Rachel had to think about it. "No," she finally decided. "But considering how much I've eaten since I've been on the cruise, I don't think my stomach knows it didn't have lunch today." And she had tried to make a practice of skipping lunch so she wouldn't find herself overeating, but it seemed only fair to put the question to him. "How about you? Are you hungry?"

Her lavender swimsuit was held in place by straps tied around her neck. One wet end was lying on the ridge of her shoulder. Taking his time to answer her question, Gard reached over and picked up the strap, studying it idly as he held it between his fingers.

"Don't you know by now, Rachel"—his voice was lowered to a husky pitch, then his darkening gaze swung slowly to her face— "that I'm starving. I don't know about you, but it's been one helluva long time between meals for me."

When he leaned toward her, Rachel began to sink back onto the stone to lie flat, her hands free to take him into her arms as he came to her. His mouth settled onto her lips with hungry need, the weight of his body moving onto her.

She slid her hands around his broad shoulders, melting under the consuming fire of his kiss. The hard skin of his ropey shoulders was warm and wet to the touch, sensual in its male strength and alive in its silken heat. There was a stir and a rush of blood through her veins; the beat of her heart lifted.

His fingers hadn't lost their hold on the end of her bathing suit strap. In an abstract way Rachel felt the slow, steady pull that untied the wet bow and relieved the pressure behind her neck. But it was the taste of him, driving full into her mouth, that dominated her senses and pushed all other sensation into secondary interest. It was the hot wetness of his mouth, the tang of tobacco on his tongue, and the salty texture of his skin that she savored.

Her hand curled its fingers into the damp, satin strands of his russet hair and pressed at the back of his head to deepen the kiss so she could absorb more of him. Soon it ceased to matter as his mouth grazed roughly over her features, murmuring her name and mixing it in with love words. There followed near delirious moments when Rachel strained to return the rain of kisses, her lips and the tip of her tongue rushing over the hard angles of his cheekbone and jaw.

Then Gard was burying his face in the curve of her neck, nuzzling her skin and taking little love bites out of the sensitive ridge of her shoulder. His tugging fingers pulled down the front of her bathing suit, freeing her breasts from the confining, elasticized material of her suit. Behind her closed eyes Rachel could see the golden fire of the sun, but when his hand caressed the ripe fullness of a breast, that radiant heat seemed to blaze within her. She was hot all over, atremble with the desires shuddering through her.

She dug her fingers into the hard flesh of his shoulders as his mouth took a slow, wandering route to the erotically erect nipple. He circled it with the tormenting tip of his tongue. Rachel arched her body in raw need, driving her shoulders onto the unyielding rock slab and feeling none of the pain, only the soaring pleasure of his devouring mouth. A building pressure throbbed within her, an ache in her loins that couldn't be satisfied by the roaming excitement of his skillful hand.

Sounds came from somewhere, striking a wrong chord in the rhapsody of the moment, only beginning to build to its crescendo. Rachel tried to isolate it from the beating of her heart and the sibilant whispers of her sawing breath.

The discordant sounds were voices—high-pitched, laughing voices. She moaned in angry protest and heard Gard swear under his breath. The weight of his body pressed more heavily onto her as if to deny the intrusion while each tried to will it away. But the voices were becoming clearer, signaling the approach of someone.

When Gard rolled from her, he caught her hands and pulled her up to sit in front of him. His broad chest and shoulders acted as a shield to conceal her seminudity in case anyone had come close enough to see them. He struggled to control the roughness of his breathing while the unbanked fires in his eyes were drawn to the swollen ripeness of her breasts and their state of high arousal.

"It sounds like we have a bunch of adventurous teenagers exploring the cascade," he said as Rachel fumbled with the straps of her suit and pulled the bodice into place.

In her passion-drugged state she lacked coordination. There was a languid weakness in her limbs and a heaviness in her eyelids. None of the inner throbbings had been satisfied, and the ache of wanting was still with her.

Gard looked in no better shape when she finally met his eyes. One side of his mouth lifted in a dryly commiserating smile. She found herself smiling back with a hint of bemusement.

"So much for the appetizer course, hmm?" he murmured and pushed to his feet. "Since our little paradise is being invaded, do you want to head back?"

"We might as well," Rachel agreed and reached for her shoes.

On the way back they passed a family with four adolescents determined to travel as far upstream as they could go. When they reached the adobe building on the bluff, Rachel didn't bother to change out of her swimming suit into her clothes. It had long since dried. She simply put on the lavender print cover-up she'd purchased instead.

"The ship isn't scheduled to sail from Puerto Vallarta until late this evening, and we still have a couple of hours of afternoon left," Gard said as the car accelerated out of the parking lot onto the paved road. "Is there anyplace you'd like to go?"

"No, I don't think so." Rachel settled back into the seat, that unsatisfied inner tension not allowing her to completely relax. "Besides, I'd rather not go anywhere when I look such a mess."

She'd had a glimpse of herself in the mirror. Her ebony hair was a black snarl of waving curls, damply defying any style, and most of her makeup had been washed off during the swim.

"You look good to me," he insisted with a sliding glance that was warm with approval.

"I'm told if you're hungry enough, anything looks good," she retorted dryly, a teasing glow in her smoky eyes.

A low chuckle came from his throat but he made no response.

There was an easy silence in the car during the long ride back to town on the twisting, coastal road, each of them privately occupied with their own thoughts. When they reached the port terminal, Gard left the car in a lot and together they walked to the ship's gangway.

"Found her, did you?" The officer on duty smiled when he recognized Gard with Rachel.

"I certainly did." There was a lightly possessive hand on her waist as he guided her onto the gangway.

After the glare and the heat of the Mexican sun, the ship seemed cool and dark when Rachel entered it, until her eyes adjusted to the change of light. Instead of taking the stairs, Gard pushed the elevator button.

"We've done enough walking and climbing for one day," he explained while they waited for it to descend to their deck. "Why don't you come to my cabin? We'll have a drink, and maybe have the steward bring us a snack."

"I'd like that," Rachel agreed. "But why don't I meet you there in half an hour? That will give me time to freshen up and change into something decent.''

''Okay. It will probably take me that long to turn the car in to the rental agency.'' The elevator doors swished open and Gard stepped to the side, allowing Rachel to enter first. ''But when you change, I'd rather you put on something 'indecent,''' he added with an engaging half-grin.

It was a little more than half an hour before Rachel knocked at the door of his cabin. With the magic of a blow-dryer and a styling brush, she had fixed her midnight-black hair into a loose and becoming style. Her simple cotton shift was grape colored, trimmed with white ribbing, and cinched at the waist with a wide white belt. Her nerves were leaping and jumping like wildfire when the door opened.

Gard's features were composed in almost stern lines, a flicker of raw impatience in the dry brown look that swept her. Before she could offer a word of greeting, he was reaching for her hand and pulling her inside to close the door.

Rachel was taken by surprise when his mouth rolled onto her lips in a hot and moist kiss. She swayed into him, feeling his hands grip her shoulders with caressing force. When he lifted his head, he had taken her breath as well as the kiss.

"What kept you?" The demand was in his eyes, but Gard tried to inject a careless note into his voice. "I was beginning to think you were going to stand me up."

"It took me longer to get ready than I thought." When his eyes ran over her and darkened with approval, Rachel was glad about the extra time she'd spent.

With the tip of his finger he located the metal pull of the hidden zipper down the front and drew it down another four inches, so the neckline gaped to show her full cleavage. The sensation licked through her veins like heat lightning. A pleased satisfaction lay dark and disturbing in his half-closed eyes.

"Now it's closer to being indecent," he murmured in soft mockery, then swung away from her to walk to the drink cabinet in the corner. "I promised you a drink. What will you have? Gin and tonic?"

"Yes." She was absurdly pleased that he remembered what she usually ordered.

While Gard fixed a drink for each of them, Rachel took the opportunity to study him unobserved. The backlight of the bar made the hard, smooth contours of his handsome features stand out in sharp relief. During that brief but exhilarating kiss she had caught the spicy scent of fresh after-shave on his skin. The cleanness of his jaw and cheek seemed to verify that he'd taken time to shave before she'd arrived. Her gaze openly admired his male body, so trimly built yet so muscular. Just looking at him was a heady stimulation all its own.

When he turned with the drinks, Rachel pretended an interest in the large sitting room, not quite ready to let him see what was in her mind. ''The room seems much larger without so many people in it,'' she remarked idly, recalling how small and crowded it had seemed at the cocktail party he'd given.

''It does,'' he agreed and handed her the glass of gin and tonic water. He raised his glass in a semblance of a silent toast and carried it to his mouth, sipping at it and looking at her over the rim, quietly assessing and measuring. ''It seems we've done this before—only last time you didn't accept the drink I offered," he said, tipping his head down as he watched the glass he lowered, then flicked a look at her through the screen of his lashes.

"Yes, the night I discovered you in my cabin," she recalled, aware of the suddenly thready run of her pulse.

"At that point it was *our* cabin." A glint of amusement shimmered in his eyes, then faded. Again some inner impatience turned him away from her. "I'll call the steward and find out what he can offer us in the way of a snack. Is there anything special you'd like?" Gard took a step toward the phone.

"I can't think of anything." She held the glass in both hands, the ice cubes transmitting some coolness to her moist palms.

That impatience became more pronounced as he stopped abruptly and swung round to face her. "It's no good, Rachel. I'm not interested in eating anything—unless it's you." The probing intensity of his dark gaze searched her face, hotly disturbing her. "You know why I asked you to my cabin. Now I want to know why you came."

The weighty silence didn't last long, but when Rachel finally spoke, her voice throbbed on a husky pitch, too emotionally charged to sound calm.

"For the same reason you asked me—because I wanted to pick up where we left off at the rock pool." But something went wrong with her certainty when she saw the unmasked flare of dark desire in his expression. As Gard took a step toward her a rush of anxiety made her half-turn away from him.

He immediately came to a halt. "What's wrong, Rachel?" It was a low, insistent demand.

Her throat worked convulsively, trying to give voice to her fears. She turned her head to look at him and forced out a nervous laugh. "I'm afraid," she admitted while trying to make light of it.

"Afraid of what?" His forehead became creased with a puzzled frown while his narrowed gaze continued to search out her face.

"I guess I'm afraid that it won't be as wonderful as I think it will," Rachel explained with a wry smile.

"Of all the—!" His stunned reaction was blatant evidence that he had expected some other explanation. The tension went out of him like an uncoiling spring. "My God, I thought it was something serious," he muttered under an expelling breath.

"I know it sounds silly—" she began.

"No, it isn't silly." In two long strides Gard was at her side, taking the glass out of her hands and setting it on a table. Then he lifted Rachel off her feet and cradled her against his chest. "It's beautiful," he said huskily as he looked down at her.

When he carried her to the bedroom door, he was so much the image of the conquering male that Rachel couldn't help smiling a little. Yet the thought was soon lost in the thrilling rush of anticipation sweeping through her veins.

Once inside the room Gard let her feet settle onto the floor, his gaze never leaving her face, locking with her eyes in a disturbing fashion. Conscious of the tripping rhythm of her pulse, she slowly dragged her gaze from his face to glance at the double bed that occupied the room.

"As soon as I saw that," Gard murmured, following her glance, "I knew I'd much rather share this cabin with you than the one we were both assigned to originally."

A comment wasn't required. Any thought of one flew away at the touch of his fingers on the front zipper of her dress. While he opened it, Rachel unfastened the belt around her waist and let it fall somewhere to the side. Gard undressed her slowly, taking her in with his eyes.

Moments later they were lying naked on the soft comfort of the double bed, facing each other. His hand made a leisurely trace of the soft, flowing lines of her breast, stomach, and hips while her fingertips made their own intimate search of his hard male contours as they loved with their eyes.

As his hands shifted to the small of her back, he applied slight pressure to gently arch her toward him. With a beginning point on her shoulder he trailed a rough pattern of nibbling kisses to the base of her throat. Rachel quivered with the wondrous sensation dancing over her skin.

"It doesn't bother me, Rachel, that I'm not the first man to love you," Gard murmured thickly into the curve of her neck. "But I'm damned well going to be the last."

Her heart seemed to leap into her throat, releasing the admission that she'd been telling him in everything but words. "I love you, Gard," she whispered achingly and turned her head to meet the lips seeking hers.

In a relatively short period of time it became apparent to Rachel that she had not underestimated how wonderful it would be in his arms. His hands and his mouth searched out every pleasure point on her body, discovering everything that excited her.

The union of their flesh came after they had become intimately familiar with each other. Nothing existed but pleasing the other, moving in rhythmic harmony, the tempo gradually increasing. It was a glorious spiraling ascent that exploded in a golden shower of sensation, unequaled in its blazing brilliance.

CHAPTER NINE

WITH HER head pillowed comfortably in the hollow of Gard's shoulder, Rachel dreamily watched the lazy trail of smoke rising from his cigarette. The bedsheet was drawn up around her hips, cool against their skin. The contentment she felt was almost a feline purring. She had no desire to move for a thousand years.

"Well?" His voice rumbled under her ear. "No comment?"

Reluctant to move, she finally tipped her head back to send him a vaguely confused glance. "About what?"

His hooded eyes looked down at her. "Did you worry for nothing?"

A sudden smile touched the corners of her mouth as Rachel realized what he was talking about. She had long ago abandoned the concern that her expectations were too high. Her head came down again.

"You know I enjoyed it," she murmured, being deliberately casual.

"Enjoyed it?" Gard taunted her mockingly. "You only *enjoyed* it? I must be losing my touch."

Her laughter was a soft sound. "Was I supposed to say I was devastated?"

"Something like that," he agreed, this time with the humor obvious in his voice, teasing her.

There was a small lull during which Gard took a last drag on his cigarette and ground out the butt in the ashtray on the stand by the bed. In that short interim Rachel's thoughts had taken her down a serious and thoughtful path.

"You know that I loved Mac," she mused aloud, sharing her thoughts with Gard. "A part of me always will. There were times, just recently, when I wondered if I would ever care so strongly for a man again. I never guessed I would love anyone like this—so totally, so—" She broke off the sentence, not finding the words to adequately express how very much she loved him.

"Don't stop," Gard chided. "Tell me more."

"You're already too conceited," Rachel accused.

"You think so?" He shifted his position, turning onto his side and taking away his shoulder as her pillow. His hand caressed her jaw and cheek as he faced her. "If I am, it's because you've made me so damned happy."

Leaning to her, he kissed her with long, drugging force. When it was over, it just added to the overall glow she felt. Her gray eyes were as soft as velvet as she gazed at him, happy and warm inside.

"Do you realize they're serving dinner, and neither one of us has had anything to eat all day?" she reminded him reluctantly, loathe to leave the bed.

"Yes," Gard said on a heavy sigh, then smiled crookedly. "But I can't say that I like the idea of sitting across the table from nosy Helen and her husband." Rachel made a little face of agreement. "I'd rather keep you all to myself. Why don't we have dinner in the cabin?"

"I'd much prefer that," she agreed huskily.

"As a matter of fact," he went further with the thought, "I can't think of any reason to leave this cabin for the next two days, until the ship puts in at Acapulco."

"I can think of one," Rachel smiled. "All my things are in my cabin. I won't have anything to wear."

"I know," he murmured with a complacently amused gleam in his eye. "It would be terrible if you had to lounge around the cabin stark naked for two days."

The thought brought a little shiver of wicked excitement. "I'm sure you'd hate that," she retorted with a playfully accusing look.

"Like a poor man hates money," Gard mocked. "But—since I don't like to share my toothbrush, I'll let you fetch some of your things tomorrow."

"Thank you," Rachel murmured with false docility.

"In the meantime"—he flipped the sheet aside and swung out of the bed—"I'll see if I can't get the steward to rustle us up something to eat.''

Rachel lay in bed a minute longer, watching him pull on his pants before walking out to the sitting room to phone. With a reluctant sigh she climbed out of bed and made use of his bathroom to wash and freshen up.

When she returned to the bedroom, instead of putting on her grape-colored shift, Rachel picked up his shirt. Its long tails reached nearly to her knees and the shoulder seams fell three inches below the point of her shoulders. The smell of him clung to the material and she hugged it tightly around her, then began to roll up the long sleeves.

There were sounds of his moving about in the sitting room. Rachel walked to the door and posed provocatively in its frame. Gard was standing in the far corner of the room by the drink cabinet.

"How do you like my robe?" she asked, drawing the rake of his glance.

"Nice." But the look in his eyes was more eloquent with approval. "I told you that you didn't need clothes."

She laughed softly and came gliding silently across the room in her bare feet to watch while he finished mixing them fresh drinks. In truth, she couldn't remember the last time she'd been so happy—or even when she'd ever been this happy. She gazed at him, so sure of her love. If she ever lost him, she thought she'd die. The possibility suddenly brought a run of stark terror to her eyes.

"Dinner is on its way, so I thought we'd have those drinks we never got around to having." He capped the bottle of tonic water and turned to hand Rachel her glass. An alertness flared in his eyes at her stricken expression. "What's the matter?"

"Nothing. I—" She started to shake her head in a vague denial, but the fear that gripped her wouldn't go away. She looked back at him. "I just have this feeling that...I'd better grab at all the happiness I can today. Tomorrow it might not be here."

A searing gentleness came into his features. He put an arm around her and brought her close against him, as if reassuring her of the hard vitality of his body. His head was bent close to her downcast face.

"Rachel, I'm not your...I'm not Mac." He corrected himself in mid-sentence, making it seem significant that he hadn't said "your husband" as he had been about to say. "Nothing's going to happen."

"I know." She stared at the scattering of silken-fine hairs on his chest, but the tightness in her throat didn't ease.

He tucked a finger under her chin and forced it up. "Do you always worry so much?" he teased to lighten her mood.

"No."

When he kissed her, she almost forgot that odd feeling, but it stayed in the back of her mind throughout the evening. It lent an urgency to her lovemaking when they went to bed that night. While Gard slept, she lay awake for a long time with the heat of his body warming her skin. In the darkness the feeling came back. It seemed like a premonition of some unknown trouble to come. Try as she might, Rachel couldn't shake it off.

STIRRING, RACHEL struggled against the drugged feeling and forced her sleep-heavy eyes to open. A shaft of sunlight was coming through the drawn curtains and laying a narrow beam on the paneled wall. There was an instant of unfamiliarity with her surroundings until she remembered that she was in Gard's cabin. Her head turned on the pillow, but the bed was empty. Unreasoning alarm shot through her, driving out the heavy thickness of unrestful sleep.

She bolted from the bed, dragging the sheet with her and wrapping it around her nude body, her hand clutching it together above a breast. She rushed to the sitting room door and pulled it open. Before she'd taken a full step inside, she halted at the sight of Hank Scarborough standing next to Gard.

Both men had turned to look when the door had been yanked open. Hank had been twirling his hat on the end of his finger, but he stopped when he saw Rachel in the door with the sheet swaddled around her. Self-consciously she lifted a hand to push at the sleep-tangle of her hair, knowing that Hank had a crystal-clear picture of the situation. Rachel hitched the sheet a little higher.

"Good morning." She broke the silence.

"Being an officer and a gentleman, I should keep my mouth shut," Hank declared with a wry shake of his head. "But if I were Gard, I'd be thinking it's a helluva good morning. And I hope I haven't embarrassed you by saying so."

"You haven't." In fact, his frankness had relaxed her. "I shouldn't have come barging in like this, but I didn't know anyone was here."

"Did you want something?" Gard asked, then slid a quick aside to his friend. "And you're right about the kind of morning it is."

"No, I—" She couldn't comfortably admit that she'd been worried that something had happened when she hadn't found Gard in bed with her—not with Hank standing there. "I just wondered what time it is."

"It's nearly ten o'clock," Gard told her.

"That late?" Her eyes widened.

"You were sleeping so soundly, I didn't have the heart to wake you," he said. "I'll order some coffee and juice."

"All right," Rachel agreed, still slightly stunned that she had slept so late. Her glance darted to Hank. "Excuse me. I think I'd better get cleaned up."

"You've missed breakfast, but we're lying off the Las Hardas Hotel," Hank informed her. "You'll be able to get breakfast at the hotel."

"Thank you." She cast him a quick smile, then moved out of the doorway and closed the door.

Her clothes were draped across a chair in the room. After she had untangled herself from the length of the sheet, Rachel hurriedly dressed. For the time being she had to be satisfied with combing her hair, because all her makeup was in her own cabin, but at least she looked presentable.

Hank had left when she returned to the sitting room. Within seconds she found herself in Gard's arms, receiving the good morning kiss he hadn't given her earlier. His stroking hands rubbed over her body when he finally drew his mouth from her clinging lips. The premonition that had troubled her so much the night before was gone, chased away by the deep glow from his searing kiss.

"You shouldn't have let me sleep so late," Rachel murmured while her fingers busied themselves in a womanly gesture of straightening the collar of his shirt.

"If Hank hadn't shown up, I planned on doing just that," Gard replied. "Although I probably would have crawled back in bed with you to do it."

"Now you tell me." She laughed and eased out of his arms. "When is the coffee coming?"

"Anytime. Why?"

"I thought I'd run down to my cabin and pick up a few things—like my toothbrush," Rachel explained, already moving toward the door.

"Don't take too long," Gard warned. "Or I'll send out a search party to find you."

Rachel had no intention of making a project of it, but even hurrying and packing only a few items she absolutely needed, plus a change of clothes, took her more than a quarter of an hour. When she returned to Gard's cabin, she had to knock twice before he came to the door.

A puzzled frown drew her eyebrows together as he opened it and immediately walked away. She had a brief glimpse of his cold and preoccupied expression.

"How come you took so long to come to the door?" she asked curiously as she quickly followed him into the room. "Is something wrong?"

"I'm on the phone to California." There was a harshness in his voice that chilled her.

Her steps slowed as she watched him walk to the phone and pick up the receiver he'd left lying on the table. A tray of cups and juice was sitting on the long coffee table in front of the sofa. Rachel changed her direction and walked over to it, sitting down so she could observe Gard.

There was very little she could piece together from his side of the conversation, but it was his body language she studied. His head was bent low in an attitude of intense interest. He kept rubbing his forehead and raking his fingers through his hair as if he didn't like what he was hearing. There was a tautness in every line.

That odd feeling began to come back, growing stronger. She poured coffee from the tall pot into a cup and sipped at it. It seemed tasteless. She folded both hands around the cup, as if needing to absorb its warmth to ward off some chill.

The phone was hung up, but his hand stayed on the receiver, gripping it tightly until his knuckles showed white. He seemed to have forgotten she was in the room.

"What is it, Gard?" Rachel asked quietly.

He stirred, seeming to rouse himself out of the dark reverie of his thoughts, and threw her a cold glance. "An emergency." He clipped out the answer and pulled his hand from the phone to comb it through his hair again.

"Is it serious?" she asked when he didn't volunteer more.

"Yes." Again his response was grudgingly given, but this time there was more forthcoming. "Bud—one of the partners in my law firm—was killed in a car accident on the freeway last night."

Even as he spoke the words, Rachel could see that he was trying to reject the truth of them. Quickly she crossed the room and gathered him into her arms. She understood that combination of shock and pain and hurt anger. His arms circled her in a crushing vice as he buried his face in the blackness of her hair.

"Damnit, he had three kids and a wife," he muttered hoarsely.

For long minutes she simply held on to him, knowing that there was no more comfort than that to give. Finally she felt the hard shudder that went through his body, and the accompanying struggle for control as he pulled his arms from around her and gripped her shoulders.

"Look..." His gaze remained downcast as he searched to pull his thoughts together. "I'm going to have to see if I can't catch a flight out of Manzanillo back to Los Angeles. Would you mind throwing my things into the suitcases?"

"I'll do it." She nodded with an outward show of calm, but inside there was a clawing panic. Last night she had worried about losing him. Today he was leaving her. They wouldn't have those two more days on the ship as he had talked about. It couldn't be over—not so quickly—not like this.

"Thanks." Gard flashed her a relieved glance and turned to pick up the phone.

Rachel bit at the inside of her lip, then boldly suggested, "Would you like me to fly back with you?"

"No." As if realizing that his rejection was slightly abrupt, Gard softened it with an explanation. "There's nothing you can do, but I appreciate the offer. It's going to be chaotic for a few days, both personally and professionally." He dialed a number and waited while it rang. "Did you say you were staying in Acapulco for a few days?"

"I was, but—I think I'll fly straight back on Saturday." She didn't look forward to those idle days in the Mexican resort city now that she knew Gard would be in Los Angeles.

"Write down your address and phone number so I can call you later next week," he said, then turned away as the party answered the phone on the other end.

While he was busy making inquiries about airline schedules and reservations, Rachel took a pen and notepad from a desk drawer and printed out her name, address, and the telephone numbers at both her home and office. She slipped it onto the table in front of Gard. He glanced at it and nodded an acknowledgment to her, continuing his conversation without a break.

A feeling of helplessness welled inside her, but there were still his suitcases to be packed. She went into the bedroom they had shared for only one night and took his suitcases from the closet and began to fill them with his clothes.

Half an hour later she was shutting and locking the last suitcase when Gard walked into the bedroom. The troubled, preoccupied expression on his features was briefly replaced with a glance of surprise at the packed suitcases on the bed.

"Are they ready to go?" he asked.

"Everything's all packed," she assured him.

"The steward's on his way." He looked at his watch. "There's an opening on a flight leaving Manzanillo in an hour and a half. If I'm lucky, I'll be able to make it and my connecting flight to Los Angeles."

As she noticed the slip of paper in his hand with her address and phone numbers marked on it, Gard folded it and slipped it into his shirt pocket. There was a knock, followed by the steward entering the cabin.

There were no more moments of privacy left to them as Gard called the steward in to take the luggage. Then they were all trooping out of the cabin and down to the lower deck to take the tender ashore.

As the collection of white block buildings tumbling down the steep sides of the mountain to the bay came closer, Rachel was conscious of the sparkling white beauty of the place, contrasted with the dark red tile roofs. Flowering bushes spilled over the sides of white balconies in scarlet profusion. But she couldn't bring herself to appreciate its aesthetic beauty. She was too conscious of Gard's thigh pressed along hers as they rode on the tender to the yacht harbor.

There was no conversation between them when they reached shore. Rachel offered to help carry one of his suitcases, but Gard refused and signaled to a hotel employee when they reached the large, landscaped pool area with its bars and dining terraces.

At the hotel lobby Gard finally stopped his hurried pace and turned to her. "I'll catch a cab to the airport from here. There's no need for you to make that ride.''

"I don't mind," she insisted, because it was just that many more minutes to spend with him.

"But I do. We'll say good-bye here so I won't have to think about you making the ride back from the airport alone," he stated.

"Okay." She lowered her gaze and tried to keep her composure under control.

"I've got your address and phone number, don't I?" There was an uncertain frown on his forehead as he began to feel in his pockets.

"It's in your shirt pocket," she assured him.

"It'll probably be the middle of the week before things settle back to normal . . . if they ever will." It was an almost cynically bitter phrase he threw on at the last, showing how deeply this loss was cutting into his life.

"I understand," she murmured, but she wanted to be with him.

"Rachel." His hand moved roughly into her hair, cupping her head and holding it while he crushed her lips under his mouth.

She slid her hands around his middle, spreading them across his back and pressing herself against the hard outline of his thighs and hips. The ache inside was a raw and painful thing, an emotional tearing that ripped at her heart.

The tears were very close when Gard dragged his mouth from hers. Rachel rested her head against his shoulder and blinked to keep them at bay. She didn't want to cry in front of him. She had never considered herself to be a weak and clinging female, but she didn't want to let him go.

It didn't seem to matter how much she tried to rationalize away this vague fear. Gard wasn't leaving her because it was what he wanted to do. There was an emergency. He had to go. Shutting her eyes for a moment, she felt the light pressure of his mouth moving over her hair.

"This is a helluva way to end our cruise," Gard sighed heavily and lifted his head, taking her by the shoulders and setting her a few inches away from him. For a moment she was the focus of his thoughts, and she could see the darkness of regret in his eyes. "We were running out of time and didn't know it."

"There will be other times," Rachel said because she needed a reassurance of that from him. There was a pooling darkness to her gray eyes, but she managed to keep back the tears and show him a calmly composed expression.

"Yes." The reassurance was absently made as Gard glanced over his shoulder to see the bellman loading his luggage into a taxi. "I'm sorry, Rachel. I have to catch that plane."

"I know." She walked with him out to the taxi, parked under the hotel's covered entrance.

There was one very brief, last kiss, a hard pressure making a fleeting impact on her lips, then Gard was striding to the open door of the taxi, passing a tip to the bellman before folding his long frame into the rear seat of the taxi.

"I'll call you," he said with a hurried wave of his hand as he shut the door.

The promise was too indefinite. She wanted to demand something more precise, a fixed time and place when he would call. Instead Rachel nodded and called, "Have a good flight!"

As the cab pulled away Gard leaned forward to say something to the driver. Rachel watched the taxi until it disappeared. If Gard looked back, she didn't see him. She had the feeling that he'd already forgotten her, his thoughts overtaken by the problems and sorrows awaiting him when he reached Los Angeles.

She turned slowly, walked back through the lobby, and descended to a dining terrace on the lower level. Out in the bay the *Pacific Princess* sat at anchor, sleek and impressive in size even at this distance. With the reflection of sun and water, the ship gleamed blue-white.

For the last six days that ship had been home to her. Its world seemed more real to her than the one in Los Angeles. The emptiness swelled within her because she was here in this world and Gard was flying to the other. But he'd call her.

Aboard ship again, Rachel was surprised to discover how many passengers knew her until she had to begin to field their inquiries about Gard. Their comments and questions varied, some expressing genuine concern and some merely being nosy.

"Where's your husband? We haven't seen him this evening," was the most common in the beginning. Then it became, "We heard there was a family emergency and your husband had to fly home. We hope it isn't serious." Only rarely was Rachel queried about her continued presence on the ship. "How come you didn't leave with him? Couldn't you get a seat on the flight?"

But there was an end to them the next day when the ship reached its destination port of Acapulco and Rachel was able to change her reservations and fly home sooner than she had originally planned.

CHAPTER TEN

THE BUZZ of the intercom phone on her desk snapped Rachel sharply out of her absent reverie. She was supposed to be reading through the stack of letters in front of her and affixing her signature to them, but the pile had only been depleted by three. Instead of reading the rest, she had been staring off into space.

Nothing seemed to receive her undivided attention anymore except the ring of the telephone. Each time it rang, at home or at the office, her heart would give a little leap, and every time she answered it, she thought this time it would be Gard.

For the last two weeks she'd lived on that hope and little else. She couldn't eat; she couldn't sleep; she was a basket case of emotions, ready to cry at the drop of a hat. Rachel was beginning to realize that this state of affairs couldn't continue. She had to resolve the matter once and for all and stop living on the edge of her nerves.

There was another impatient buzz of the intercom. No light was blinking to indicate that a phone call was being held on the line for her. Rachel picked up the receiver.

"Yes, Sally, what is it?" she asked her secretary with grudging patience.

"Fan Kemper is here to see you," came the answer. "She says she's taking you to lunch."

After a second's hesitation Rachel simply replied, "Send her in."

Before she had returned the receiver to its cradle, the door to her private office was opened and Fan came sweeping in, exuding energy and bright efficiency. A smile beamed from her friend's face, but there was a critical look in her assessing glance.

"Sorry, Fan, but I can't have lunch with you today," Rachel said and began to write her signature on the letters she should have already signed.

"I know I'm not down on your appointment book, but I thought I'd steal you away from the office." Fan crossed to the desk, undeterred by the refusal. "I've only seen you once since you came back from the cruise— and every time I phone you, we never talk more than five minutes because you're expecting some 'important call.'"

"I had a lot of catching up to do when I came back." It was a vague explanation, accompanied by an equally vague smile in her friend's direction.

"You look awful," Fan announced.

"Thanks." Rachel laughed without amusement.

"You're lucky you got some sun on that cruise. Without that tan those circles under your eyes would really be noticeable." Fan pulled a side chair closer to the desk and sat in it, leaning forward in an attitude that invited confidence. "You might as well tell me, Rachel. Hasn't he called?"

The "he" was Gard, of course. When she had returned from vacation and seen the Kempers, Rachel had mentioned him. Fan, being Fan, had read through the lines and knew instinctively that the relationship hadn't been as casual as Rachel had tried to imply.

"No, he hasn't called," she admitted, grimly concealing the hurt.

"It's possible he lost your number," Fan reasoned. "And unless he knows your company is called the Country House, he won't be able to find you, since your home number is unlisted."

"I know."

During the last two weeks she'd had countless arguments with herself. She'd come up with all sorts of reasons to explain why Gard hadn't called her as he'd promised, but she could never forget the possibility that he wasn't interested in seeing her again.

True, he'd said a lot of things to lead her to believe otherwise. But men often said things in the heat of passion that meant nothing on reexamination. Pride insisted it had just been a holiday affair, intense while it lasted, but best forgotten by her.

"Rachel, how long are you going to eat your heart out over him before you do something about it?" Fan wanted to know.

"About twenty more minutes," Rachel replied calmly with a glance at her watch.

"What?" Fan sat up straight and blinked at her.

There was a dry curve to Rachel's mouth as she met her friend's puzzled gaze. "That's why I can't go to lunch with you. I'm going to his office this afternoon." She had looked up his name in the telephone directory so many times that she knew his address and phone number by heart. "I have to know where I stand once and for all."

Fan leaned back in her chair and released a sighing breath of satisfaction. "I'm so glad to hear you say that. Would you like me to come with you and lend a little moral support?"

"No. I have to do this on my own," Rachel stated.

"Have you called?" Fan wondered. "Did you make an appointment to see him?"

"No. I thought about it," she admitted. "But if he doesn't want to see me anymore, I didn't want to be pawned off by his secretary or have some impersonal conversation with him on the phone. When I talk to him, I want to be able to see his face." She slashed her name across the last letter. "So I'm just going over to his office and take the chance that he'll be in.''

"If he isn't?" Fan studied her with gentle sympathy.

"I don't know." Rachel sighed heavily. "Then I guess it's back to square one."

"John knows him—or least they've met before," Fan reminded her. "I could always have him come up with some excuse to call him and mention in passing that you are one of John's clients—use the name coincidence that started this whole thing. At least John could find out what his reaction is."

"Thanks." She appreciated her friend's offer to help, but she didn't feel it was right to have them solve her problems. "I'd rather do this without involving you and John."

"If you change your mind, just tell me," Fan insisted, standing up to leave. "And you'd better call me later, because I'll be sitting by the phone on pins and needles."

"I will," Rachel promised with a more natural smile curving her mouth and watched her friend leave, spending an idle minute reminding herself how lucky she was to have a friend like Fan Kemper.

AT HALF past one that afternoon Rachel stood outside the entrance to the suite of offices in the posh Wilshire Boulevard address and had cause to wish for the moral support Fan had offered. Her knees felt shaky and her stomach was emptily churning.

The elaborately carved set of double doors presented a formidable barrier to be breached. On the wall beside them there was a rich-looking plaque with brass letters spelling out MACKINLEY, BROWN & THOMPSON, ATTOR-NEYS-AT-LAW.

A cowardly part of her wanted to turn and walk away, so she could believe a little longer in the variety of excuses she had made to herself on Gard's behalf. Squaring her shoulders, Rachel breathed a deep, steadying breath and reached for a tall brass doorgrip. The door swung silently open under the pull of her hand and she stepped onto the plush pile carpeting of the reception area.

The young girl at the switchboard looked up when she entered and smiled politely. "May I help you?"

"I'd like to see Mr. MacKinley—Mr. Gardner MacKinley," Rachel clarified her answer in case there was more than one MacKinley in the firm.

"Is he expecting you?" the girl inquired.

"No, he isn't, but I need to see him." Which was the truth.

As she punched a set of interoffice numbers, she asked, "What name shall I give him?"

Rachel hesitated, then replied, using her maiden name, "Miss Hendrix." She'd rather he didn't know who she was until he saw her.

She listened while the girl relayed the information. "Yes, Mr. MacKinley, this is Cindy at the reception desk. There's a Miss Hendrix here to see you. She doesn't have an appointment but she says she needs to speak with you." Rachel held her breath during the pause. "I'll tell her. Thank you." The girl pushed another button to end the connection and looked at Rachel with another polite smile. "He's tied up at the moment, but he expects to be free shortly. If you'd care to have a seat, you're welcome to wait."

"Thank you." It was one more hurdle cleared, but the tension increased as Rachel walked over to sit in one of the leather-covered armchairs against a paneled wall.

Three wide hallways led in separate directions from the reception area. Rachel had no idea which one led to Gard's office. Her chair was positioned beside the opening to one of them and provided her a view of the other two. Her heart was thumping in her chest, louder than the clock ticking on the wall. She watched the clicking rotation of the second hand, then realized that would not make the time pass more quickly. She picked up a magazine lying on a walnut table and nervously began to flip through it.

The cords in her neck were knotted with tension and her nerves were stretched raw. Tremors of apprehension were attacking her insides, adding to the overall strain. From the hallway behind her she caught the sound of a woman's low voice, indifferent to the words until a man's voice responded and the man was Gard. Recognition of his voice splintered through her, nearly driving her out of the chair so she could face the sound of his approaching voice.

Through sheer self-control Rachel forced herself to remain seated. The instant he appeared in her side vision, her gaze slid to his familiar form. His mahogany dark hair and muscularly tapered build were exactly the same as she remembered.

She hardly paid any attention at all to the woman he was walking to the door with until she noticed that Gard had his arm around her. Rachel took another look at the woman, feeling her heart being squeezed by jealous pain, and saw how young and wholesomely attractive she was with her gleaming chestnut hair and adoring brown eyes.

Gard's back was to her when he stopped by the door, giving Rachel a clear view of the woman who had his hand on her waist. In her numbed state it took her a minute to realize the pair were talking. She wanted to cry out when she heard what Gard was saying.

"I'll come over to your place for dinner tonight, then afterward I'm taking you to the Schubert Theater. I pulled some strings and got tickets for tonight's performance. I know you've been wanting to see the play."

"I have," the woman admitted, then bit at her lips and frowned. "What do you think I should wear?"

Gard had taken hold of the woman's hand and was now raising it to his mouth, pressing a warm kiss on the top of it while he eyed her. "A smile," he suggested.

"And nothing else, I suppose." The woman laughed. "Advice like that could get a girl in trouble." She leaned up and kissed him lightly. "I'll see you tonight."

"I'll come early, so pour me a scotch about six o'clock." He pushed open the door and held it for her while she walked through.

Pain was shattering Rachel's heart into a thousand pieces, immobilizing her. Raw anguish clouded her gray eyes, which couldn't tear their gaze from him. When Gard turned away from the door, his idle glance encountered that look.

His dark eyes narrowed in frowning astonishment before a smile began to spread across his features. "Rachel." There was rough warmth in the way he said her name, then he took a step toward her.

It was too much to see that light darkening his eyes when not a moment before he had been flirting with another woman. Rage followed hot on the heels of her pain. She had wanted to know where she stood with him and now she knew—in line!

Rachel pushed out of the chair and aimed for the door, intent on only one thing—leaving before she made a complete fool of herself. But Gard moved quickly into her path and caught hold of her shoulders.

"What are you doing here?" He held on when she tried to twist out of his grasp, pushing at his arms with her hands.

"I came to find out why you hadn't called," she admitted with bitter anger that slid into sarcasm. "I saw the reason."

"What are you talking about?" he demanded, giving her a hard shake when she continued to struggle.

A glaze of tears was stinging her eyes. She glared through it at the angry and impatient expression chiseled on his features.

"I don't care to take up any more of your valuable time," she flashed bitterly. "I'm sure you have a lot to do before you can keep your dinner engagement tonight.''

As understanding dawned in his eyes, they darkened with exasperation. ''It isn't what you're thinking. Brenda is Bud's wife, the partner I just lost. She's lonely and needs company.''

''Especially at night,'' Rachel suggested, untouched by his explanation. ''Consoling widows must be your specialty.''

She nearly succeeded in wrenching free of his hands, but he caught her again and turned her around, half pushing and half carrying her along with him as he headed for the hallway by her chair. The receptionist was watching them with wide-eyed wonder, a silent and curious observer of the virulent scene being played out before her.

''You are going to listen to my explanation whether you like it or not,'' Gard informed her in an angrily low voice as he marched her past a secretarial pool and a short row of offices.

''Well, I don't like it, and I'm not interested in hearing anything you have to say!'' she hissed, conscious of the curious looks they were receiving. She stopped resisting him rather than draw more attention.

"That's too bad," he growled and pushed her into a large, executive-styled office with windows on two sides and a healthy collection of potted plants. "Because you're going to hear it anyway." The door was shut with a resounding click of the latch.

The minute he let go of her, Rachel moved to the center of the room and stopped short of the long oak desk. She was hurting inside and it showed in the wary gray of her eyes. When he came toward her, she stiffened noticeably. His mouth thinned into a grim line and he continued by her to the desk. He picked up the phone and pushed a button.

"Tell Carol to come in and give me a report on her progress so far," Gard instructed and hung up.

Turning, he leaned against the desk and rested a hip on the edge of it. His level gaze continued to bore into Rachel as he folded his arms and waited silently. Long seconds later there was a light rap on the door.

"Come in." He lifted his voice, granting permission to enter.

A young brunette, obviously Carol, walked in with a pen and notepad in her hand. Her glance darted to Rachel, then swung apprehensively to her employer.

"I'm sorry, but I still haven't been able to locate her," she began her report with an apology. "A couple of people have recognized the name as someone in the business, but they couldn't refer me to anyone. I'm almost through the L's in the Yellow Pages. I never realized there were so many furniture stores in the metropolitan area of Los Angeles."

It was Rachel's turn to stare at Gard, searching his face to make sure she was placing the right meaning on all this. A look of hard satisfaction mixed with the anger smoldering in his eyes.

"Thank you, Carol," he said to the young girl. "You don't have to make any more calls."

"Sir?" She looked worried that he was taking the task from her because she hadn't made any progress.

"Since you've spent so much time on this, I thought you should meet Rachel Mac-Kinley." Gard gestured to indicate Rachel.

"You found her!" Her sudden smile of surprise was also partly relief.

"Yes." He let the girl's assumption stand for the time being while his gaze remained on Rachel. "By the way, Rachel, would you mind telling Carol the name of your furniture company?"

It was suddenly very difficult to speak. Her throat was all tight with emotion. It was obvious that Gard had been looking for her, but she still had some doubts about what that meant.

"The Country House." She supplied the name in a voice that was taut and husky.

"The T's." The girl shook her head in faint amazement.

"Thank you, Carol. That will be all." Gard dismissed the girl. There was another long silence while she exited the private office. "Now do you believe that I've been trying to locate you?" he challenged when they were alone again.

"Yes." It seemed best to keep her answer simple and not jump to any more conclusions.

"I jotted my flight schedules on the back of the slip of paper you gave me with your address and phone numbers on it. It was late when I arrived back in L.A. I didn't pay close attention to what was in my shirt pockets when I emptied them. All I saw were the flight schedules on the paper. I didn't need them anymore, so I threw the paper away. It wasn't until a couple of days later when I was looking for your phone number that I realized what had happened. By then my cleaning lady had already been in and emptied the wastebaskets."

The explanation was delivered in a calm, relatively flat voice. It was a statement of fact that told Rachel nothing about his feelings toward her. Nothing in his look or his attitude offered encouragement.

"I see," she murmured and lowered her gaze to the beige carpet, searching its thick threads as if they held a clue.

"Information informed me that you had a private, unlisted number, so that only left me with the fact that you owned a furniture company," Gard stated. "I pulled one of the junior typists out of the pool and had her start to phone all the stores listed under the furniture section of the Yellow Pages and ask for you."

"I thought it was possible that you had somehow lost my number," Rachel admitted slowly. "That's why I came by today."

"But you also thought it was possible that I didn't *intend* to call you," he accused.

There was a defiant lift of her chin as she met his unwavering gaze. "It was possible."

His chest expanded on a deep, almost angry breath that was heavily released. Gard looked away from her for an instant, then slid his glance back.

"I won't ask you why you thought it was possible. I'm liable to lose my temper and break that pretty neck of yours," he muttered, his jaw tightly clenched. "Is it fair to say that you understand why I haven't called you before now?"

"Yes." Rachel nodded.

"Good." Unfolding his arms, he straightened from the desk. "Now, let's see if we can't clear up this matter about Brenda."

"I'd rather just forget it," she insisted, her breath running deep and agitated. "It's none of my business."

"To a point, you're absolutely right. And if you hadn't insulted Brenda by the implication of your accusations against me, I wouldn't explain a damned thing to you," he informed her roughly. "She buried her husband last week. She puts up a good front, but she's hurting and lonely. Damnit, you should know the feeling! There are times when it helps her to have people around her who were close to Bud. He was my friend as well as my law partner."

"I'm sorry." Rachel felt bad about the thoughts she'd had when she'd seen Gard with that attractive woman—and the things she'd said, out of hurt, when he had explained who the woman was. "I jumped to the wrong conclusion."

"You couldn't have jumped to that conclusion if you hadn't already decided that I didn't care about seeing you again,'' he countered.

"I hadn't decided that," she denied.

"I'd forgotten," Gard eyed her lazily. "You were prepared to give me the benefit of reasonable doubt. That's why you came to see me, isn't it?"

"Something like that, yes!" Rachel snapped, not liking the feeling of being on the witness stand. "You could have lost my number and I had to know!"

"Yet you were also willing to believe that I had just been stringing you along during the cruise, and that I didn't have any feelings toward you."

"It was possible," she insisted. "How could I be sure what kind of man you are? I haven't known you that long."

"How long do you have to know someone before you can love them?" Gard demanded, coming over to stand in front of her. "Two weeks? Two months? Two years? I recall distinctly that you said you loved me. Didn't you mean it?"

"Yes." Reluctantly she pushed the angry word out.

"Then why is it so hard for you to accept that I love you?" he challenged.

She flashed him a resentful look. "Because you never said you did."

He stared at her for a long minute. "I must have said it at least a thousand times—every time I looked at you and touched you and held you." The insistence of his voice became intimately low.

"You never said it," Rachel repeated with considerably less force. "Not in so many words."

His eyes lightened with warm bemusement as a smile curved his lips. "Rachel, I love you," he said as if repeating it by rote. "There you have it 'in so many words.'"

It hurt almost as much for him to say the words without any feeling. She started to turn away. A low chuckle came from his throat as his arms went around her and gathered her into their tightening circle. She started to elude his mouth but it closed on her lips too quickly.

The persuasive ardor of his warm, possessive kiss melted away her stiffness. Her hands went around his neck as she let the urgency of loving him sweep through her. With wildly sweet certainty Rachel knew she had come home. She lived in the love he gave her, which completed her as a person the same way her love completed him.

"You crazy little fool," he muttered near her ear while he kept her crushed in his arms. "I was half in love with you from the beginning. It didn't take much of a push to make me fall the rest of the way."

"You knew even then?" She pulled back a little to see his face because she found it incredible that he could have been so sure of his feelings almost from the start.

"Admit it," he chided her. "We were attracted to each other from the beginning. You saw me when I arrived, just the same way I noticed you sitting there outside the terminal."

"That's true," Rachel conceded.

"When you came strolling into what I thought was my cabin and claimed to be Mrs. Gardner MacKinley, I thought it was some practical joke of Hank's and he'd put you up to the charade. Despite your convincing talk about the reissued ticket, I still didn't believe you until you became so indignant at the thought of sharing the cabin with me. I could tell that wasn't an act.''

"And I couldn't understand how you could take it all so lightly,'' she remembered.

"That's just about the time I started to tumble,'' Gard informed her, brushing his mouth over her cheek and temple as if he didn't want to break contact with her even to talk. "I was intrigued by the idea of sharing a cabin with you and fascinated by the thought that you were Mrs. Gardner MacKinley. I didn't even want to correct people when they mistook you for my wife.''

"Neither did I,'' she admitted, laughing at the discovery that he'd felt the same.

"Remember the cocktail party?'' He nibbled at the edge of her lips while his hands tested the feel of her body arched to his length.

"Yes,'' she murmured.

"When I introduced you as Mrs. Mac-Kinley, that's when I knew for certain that was who I wanted you to be—my wife. She was no longer some faceless woman I hadn't met. She was you—standing in the same room

with me—and already possessing my name."
He lifted his head about an inch above her
lips. "Are you convinced now that I love
you?"

"Yes." She was filled with the knowledge,
its golden light spreading through every inch
of her body.

"Then let's make it legal before something
else separates us," he urged.

"I couldn't agree more."

"It's about time," he muttered and covered her mouth with a long kiss, not giving
her a chance to worry about anything but
loving him.

"I'M NOT GOING TO APOLOGIZE

because I have the normal urge to take you in my arms and kiss you."

She looked at him, but said nothing. She could feel the vein throbbing in her neck, its hammering beat betraying how his seductive voice disturbed her. She was conscious of his closeness, the hand that came to rest on the curve of her waist, and the steadiness of his gaze.

"And if the kiss lived up to my expectations, I would probably be tempted to press it further," he admitted calmly. "It's natural. After all, what's wrong with a man wanting to take a woman into his arms and kiss her? For that matter, what's wrong with a woman wanting to kiss a man?"